THE LEGEND OF
JACK RIDDLE

by H. Easson

STONE ARCH BOOKS
a capstone imprint

The Legend of Jack Riddle is published by Stone Arch Books
A Capstone Imprint
1710 Roe Crest Drive
North Mankato, Minnesota 56003
www.mycapstone.com

Library of Congress Cataloging-in-Publication Data is available on
the Library of Congress website.

ISBN 978-1-4965-5408-6 (hardcover)
ISBN 978-1-4965-5409-3 (eBook PDF)

Summary: Twelve-year-old Jack finds himself caught up in a real, live
fairy tale and discovers that they're not the cutesy stories he thought
they were. With the help of a mysterious professor at his school, he
must outsmart the evil Gretel before her cruel spell traps him forever.

Book design by Kay Fraser

Cover and interior illustrations by Davide Ortu

Printed and bound in the United States of America.
010748S18

For David, who always believed in me.

TURN BACK WHILE YOU STILL CAN.

STILL HERE? WELL, DON'T SAY
I DIDN'T WARN YOU.

So you think you know about fairy tales?
All those handsome princes, slushy princesses
living happily ever after . . . blah, blah, bleugh.

You don't. You've been lied to.

Real fairy tales HAVE CLAWS. They reach out
from the page and GRAB YOU BY THE THROAT.

COME A LITTLE CLOSER.

Don't worry. Just because I have BIG TEETH
doesn't mean I bite.

Well, only sometimes.

Warm yourself by the fire. Let the heat from
the crackling flames thaw your numb fingers.
Yes, I do have a cozy cave, don't I? Solid
limestone. It keeps me safe from the forest
outside. It's so chilly out there, with the wind
rushing past your face. Almost feels like you
could freeze to death, doesn't it?

I know why you're here. You want to know about the ancient stories, the ones your parents never told you. That's awfully brave of you. People never come to visit. They stay away from CREATURES like me.

Take my hand. I know, I KNOW, MY CLAWS ARE SHARP, but I'll try not to scratch.

Are you sure you still want to go?
I can't promise to keep you safe.

REALLY?

Then let's go and look outside. Pull your coat a little tighter. We're going somewhere even colder. This tale starts at midnight in the seventeenth century. A witch is about to be hanged — and we don't want to miss that.

CHAPTER 1

THE GINGERBREAD WITCH

The year 1610

Gretel lay in front of the dying fire and listened to the muffled church bells. They rang through the night, reaching her in the tiny one-roomed shack. Her whole family lay sleeping around her and their snores were thick in the smelly air. She counted the bells silently in her head. *Nine, ten, eleven, twelve.* She smiled.

Midnight.

She slipped out from under the threadbare blanket and stood up, shivering. Quiet as a ghost, she tiptoed past the slumbering bodies on the floor.

"Mmmmmmuuummpph?"

Gretel froze and held her breath. Her little sister — one of six — lay next to her feet. The young girl had stirred when Gretel tried to edge past her. But no, she was still sleeping, her mouth hanging open.

Gretel let out a small sigh of relief.

Reaching the front door, she lifted the bolt and slipped into the woods outside.

She walked quickly through the trees, using the moonlight to find her way. Frost crunched in the grass beneath her bare feet, and she shivered in her thin woolen dress. But Gretel needed to reach the village before daybreak.

She really wanted a good seat to watch the hanging.

* * *

After half an hour, she reached the boundary of the forest. In front of her was an ancient wooden gate. She grasped the top, feeling its pitted, rough surface. She pulled it to one side and stepped into the village. The gate groaned and slammed shut behind her.

She walked across the cobblestones, ignoring the sharp edges on her cold feet. In front of her, right in the middle of the village square, was her destination.

The hangman's gallows.

But she hesitated when she saw the wooden structure loom before her. A twisted rope hung from the top and a wicked-looking noose was attached to the end.

She stared at it with a mixture of fear and fascination. It hadn't been there the day before. But the villagers had all heard the thump of the workmen's hammers and knew what was being built and why. The Gingerbread Witch would hang the next day.

The wind suddenly whistled through the square, making

the wooden boards creak and moan. Gretel gasped as the rope swung slowly in the breeze. It looked like it was reaching for her.

But she lifted her chin and walked stubbornly to the foot of the platform.

"Ain't nothin' or nobody gonna stop me from seein' this," she whispered into the deserted square.

There was a high-pitched giggle from the trees behind her.

She froze. What if it was the fairy folk? She was here all alone with them at night.

Gretel was terrified of the fairy folk. They were evil little monsters who curdled the cows' milk and stole children. She didn't want the fairy folk to take her away. But nothing happened — there was only the whistling wind.

Carefully she crept underneath the gallows and sat down at the back, far from sight. Pulling her dress down over her knees for warmth, she settled down to wait for dawn.

* * *

Gretel was woken by the sound of shouting a few hours later. Stiff from sleeping in the cold, she rubbed the grit from her eyes and peered out from her hiding place under the gallows.

A crowd had gathered in the village square and the sun had now risen. There were no real roads in the village, just decades of mud and horse manure trampled down until the ground was solid. Unless it rained — then the villagers squelched through ankle-deep stinking sewage. (Most of them didn't own a toilet, so they just tipped their leavings into the street.)

Luckily today the filthy ground was frozen solid and covered in a fine veil of frost. The villagers huddled together as they headed to the gallows. Excitement flowed through the crowd and several children skipped around the edges.

The hanging was about to begin.

The crowd roared. Gretel peered through the cracks in the wood and saw a group of soldiers heading toward her. They were dragging the woman known as the Gingerbread Witch to the gallows.

Gretel made a squeaking noise and clapped her hands over her mouth to muffle the sound. She heard the *clump-clump* of the soldiers' heavy boots as they walked up the stairs over her head. She craned her neck and looked up through the slats, just in time to see the woman thrown to her knees directly above Gretel.

The rope swung sluggishly in the breeze above the woman, who knelt, stunned, beneath it.

Gretel gazed upward in awe. She'd never seen a witch up close before. The witch's hair was a pure white-blond. She had sad, gentle brown eyes, which stared at the crowd from a thin face.

Gretel heard a rustling from the crowd and looked back through the cracks to see what was happening now. A man wearing a fancy suit made of black velvet and a large three-cornered hat strode through the crowd. It parted respectfully to let him through. Gretel frowned, then realized who he was — the town mayor.

The mayor walked solemnly to the foot of the gallows. He cleared his throat and unraveled a scroll of yellowed parchment. In a booming voice, he read out the woman's crime: "She has been found guilty of witchcraft!"

The crowd gasped and pressed in closer, the better to see the wretched woman. The noise level rose as they muttered among themselves.

A filthy man with a glass eye whispered, "I always knew it, I did, I tells you. I saw her, clear as day, with me own eye, feeding people potions." He paused and scratched one of the fleas in his hair. "Or was it potatoes . . . ?"

People bobbed their heads in agreement and started to swap stories about the evil things the woman had done — or, at least, what they'd *heard* she'd done, which in their minds was the same thing. Their whispers mixed together and strange stories floated on the wind.

The mayor's lips twitched in irritation.

Gretel gave a muffled laugh. It was obvious he didn't like being ignored.

Bowing his head, the mayor carried on reading. "Therefore, she has been sentenced to die today." He paused, then said dramatically, "By hanging."

The crowd started to cheer. "BURN 'ER INSTEAD!" someone screamed.

The mayor smiled. Everyone was staring at him now, their mouths open in wonder.

"NO!" screeched a woman with ruddy cheeks and chapped hands. "THROW 'ER IN A BARREL WITH A SNAKE, A RAT, AND A DOG!"

A man with a bushy mustache and huge sideburns shook his head. "NO, NO, GIVE 'ER A CHANCE! Try an' drown her! If she floats, she's guilty. If she dies, well . . ." He shrugged.

The mayor was clearly not happy. No one was listening to him again! He scowled and stomped his foot on the ground, dislodging a piece of frozen, smelly mud. It flew into the crowd and smacked a young boy on the nose, making him cry out with disgust. The crowd fell silent and sulked.

"Hear this," the mayor shouted. "She shall hang today, right now, for her crimes! The witch-finder has found her guilty." He drew a breath. "So she dies."

The crowd roared its approval and the executioner strode onto the wooden platform of the gallows. Gretel peered up from the shadows below.

The executioner pulled the noose over the witch's head. "Any last words?" he asked, the black mask he wore muffling his voice.

The woman raised her head and slowly lifted her eyes to the people screaming for her death.

The crowd gasped and backed away. Gretel knew they

were wondering why he was letting the witch speak. She could curse them all!

The woman spoke in a painful, raspy croak. "I leave to ye a prophecy. Only by understanding how to fulfill it, can thy children be saved from the evil that will be let loose when I am dead. Listen well and listen carefully . . ."

The crowd became uneasy and people shivered at her words. Most would have run away, but they couldn't resist staying to hear a wicked tale.

The woman raised her voice to speak above the frightened whispers of the people. They leaned forward expectantly.

Gretel held her breath, hoping to hear about evil spirits — who, as everybody knew, danced the muddy roads at night, wearing crowns made of dead ravens.

But instead the witch said, "First comes the goblin, then the witch. Destruction will rain down on thy children's heads. It will be thus for several hundred years . . ." The woman paused. The wind could be heard blowing mournfully through the village square. ". . . Unless water and spirit bring fire to the place where earth and air meet."

With a grunt, the executioner spat on the ground.

Gretel rolled her eyes. She'd heard better speeches, and scarier ones too.

The crowd booed. "Kill her!" they shrieked. "Burn the wicked Gingerbread Witch!"

But the mayor just scowled this time in annoyance at the delay. He'd thought it would be all over by now. He had a lovely breakfast on the table at home. He could imagine the steaming eggs and bacon going cold. Not to mention his wife's disapproval at his lateness. And the way she would hold the rolling pin threateningly. She had a nasty tendency to hit him over the head with it when she was displeased.

Impatiently, the mayor nodded at the hooded executioner.

"No, please wait for the sake of thy children's souls!" cried the woman. "I have not yet finished telling ye about the prophecy! Water and spirit must bring fire to the place where earth and air meet, which means —"

The executioner stepped forward and pushed the witch off the wooden platform. She gave a terrible shriek that was cut short as the rope unraveled, flew to its full length, and cracked to a halt.

The dead woman swung gently above the heads of the crowd. Her shadow fell over Gretel, hiding below in the gloom. She stared at the witch's slim feet pointing toward the ground, beneath her woolen dress.

Tears of happiness fell down Gretel's cold cheeks. *At last!* she thought, *the Gingerbread Witch is dead.* A small grin lit up her face and she punched the air silently. *Long live the NEW WITCH!*

CHAPTER 2
JACK RIDDLE

Present day

Jack Riddle was bored. Extremely bored. He'd been on the train for three hours, and it had not sped up once. *It just carries on chug-ruddy-chugging through the hills,* he thought moodily.

He sighed and sat back in his seat, listening to the steady creak and hum of the train as it made its way through the darkness. He turned to the window and watched his glum face in the reflection. The dim outline of dark trees could be seen through his features. He was unusually small for his twelve years, with blond hair that stuck straight up like a brush. Skinny as a twig, he gave the impression of being all knobbly knees and elbows. A smattering of freckles lay across the bridge of his nose and an obstinate chin reflected back at him in the window.

He sighed again, much more loudly, making the other man in the car rustle his newspaper in annoyance. Even though he was getting to miss a few days of school, Jack wanted to be back in Manchester, not on his way to Sheffield. But his mom had bundled him onto the train, ignoring his protests, and shoved a ham sandwich in one hand and a can of soda in the other. The sandwich had long since been eaten. Its remains lay on the seat next to him, giving off the metallic smell of old meat.

Jack pulled his phone from his pocket and checked the signal. Nothing. Not even a hint of a bar. Jack felt panic start to seize him. What was he going to do without his phone? Like most of his friends, he was glued to it. He didn't like it sometimes — it meant his mom and dad could get hold of him whenever they wanted — but the phone was his life. He used it to pass the time in class when he was bored, watch videos, buy stuff online when he had money, and chat with his hundreds of friends on social media. (Well, people who'd asked to be his friend. He wasn't *friends* with them all really; that would be silly.) Basically, it was his best friend. His mom and dad joked that he must even sleep with the phone under his pillow. Jack told them not to be daft. He slept with it next to his lamp, within easy reach.

He took a picture of the nearly empty train and tried to send it to his friend Ayo. But with a feeling of dread, he watched as the little screen flickered and died. Was the battery dead?

Without warning the train shuddered to a halt. The brakes screeched and the wheels slid on the tracks, then all was quiet. Jack pressed his nose to the window and stared at the gloomy station outside. An old, battered sign spotted with mud said GRIMBLEDYKE.

Jack stood up, grabbed his suitcase, then made his way to the door of the train. The doors slid open and he stepped onto the platform, cursing as he staggered from the long drop to the ground. He really hoped he'd start growing more. Everyone else in his year at school was at least six inches taller than him — and that was just the girls. His height was starting to get embarrassing. He made a mental note to Google growth spurts when he finally got Internet access.

Clicking his tongue, Jack turned around to see where the exit was. But there was no light anywhere in the station, not even a streetlamp. He turned around in panic as the train chugged away. It seemed so comforting, all lit up like a Christmas tree. When the back end of the train had gone around a bend and was out of view, Jack took a tentative step forward in the dark, hoping he was facing the station building and was not about to step off the tracks.

"Hello?" he shouted. "Is anyone there?"

A gruff voice pitted with age rasped back from the darkness, "What do ye want?"

Jack thought it should be pretty obvious what he wanted, with a flashlight being high up on his list of priorities. "Er, well, I need to get to a house called Salem's Cottage. It's supposed to be somewhere near this station?"

There was no reply. The silence grew thicker.

Just when Jack thought he was chatting to an extremely talented animal, the voice came again. "If ye really want to go there, then it's down yonder lane."

A face appeared out of the night. Jack yelped. It was a bald old man, with no front teeth and eyes like a weasel. He wore a faded blue uniform and a stationmaster's cap.

The stationmaster pointed behind Jack. Frowning, Jack turned around. By now his eyes had adjusted to the dark and he could see a soft swirl of mist hanging above a gravel road. *Fantastic,* he thought sourly.

The stationmaster rasped, "Whatever ye do, don't accept any gifts from the wench."

Jack was about to ask what he meant, but when he turned back, the man had disappeared.

* * *

What felt like hours later, Jack was still walking along the winding path and dragging his suitcase behind him, which kept getting stuck in the mud. He cursed his bad luck. Why did he have to visit the middle of nowhere? Everyone else in his class got to go on real holidays, like to Jamaica and Spain.

But nooooo, he had to visit his aunt. His mom said he couldn't go abroad anyway because they couldn't afford it that year.

Jack stomped angrily through the soupy mud, not caring how much was splattering up the backs of his legs. He'd already ruined his best sneakers on the path, which was inches deep in oozing muck.

He rounded a corner and stopped. The muddy path led to an iron gate topped with two stone gargoyles. They had their mouths open in silent screams. Beyond the gate was a rundown old cottage surrounded by an ancient forest.

Jack thought he would feel relieved to see the cottage after his long walk, but for some reason he didn't want to move. The thought of walking up to that creepy house was enough to make him want to turn around and walk all the way back through the dark to the train station. Telling himself not to be such a baby, he shrugged away his fears and continued to walk toward the cottage, which was covered in wild tendrils of ivy that climbed over the faded bricks. It had a pointed roof and tiny windows that glowed with a dim red light. Several ravens nested on one side of the roof, and the air was filled with their harsh, barking calls. A crooked chimney spilled out billows of smoke, which lazily floated toward Jack.

Well, fire means people, he thought.

He huffed his way toward the cottage, hauling his suitcase behind him. The wheels bumped along, getting stuck every few feet in the mud. By the time Jack passed the two gargoyles (stopping to pat one on the head) and reached the front door, he was gulping for breath. After waiting a minute to compose himself, he lifted his hand and grasped the door knocker. It was made of brass and shaped like a man's face, with a gaping mouth and long, sharp teeth.

Jack raised his eyebrows, swallowed his misgivings, and knocked.

The knocker boomed loudly and made Jack jump. No one came. After waiting awhile with chattering teeth, Jack lifted the knocker again. But before he could hit it, the door swung inward, pulling Jack into the house.

"Oomph," he gasped. He righted himself and gazed up at the person in the doorway. Jack's heart beat faster as he tried to make out the inhumanly tall figure. The light from inside blinded him, and he could only see the outline of the figure standing in front of him. Most people were tall compared to Jack, but this was odd. The person had a very tall *head*.

Please let this be the wrong house, he thought.

A mouth in the dark face opened, then a voice as sickly as syrup in the morning cried, "Hello! Oh Jackie-poo, I thought it was you! How's my dear great-great-great-GREAT niece, your mother, doing? Is she still with that scoundrel, your father? Oh dearie me — look at you, you're shivering. Aren't I a nasty beast keeping you out in this damp weather? Come inside, where it's warm and toasty."

Jack slumped in relief at the sound of his great-great . . . (whatever . . . his math was terrible) aunt's voice. He'd heard that sugary sound on the telephone when his mom had arranged his visit here. She'd wanted him to finally meet his long-lost — and very old — Aunt Gee Gee. At least, he thought that was how you said it. None of his family had ever met her. She always sent birthday and Christmas cards, signed in an illegible scrawl. The cards were politely put on the mantelpiece and letters of thanks were dutifully returned.

His mother would tut and say it was such a shame they never had the time to visit Aunt Gee Gee, especially as she must be getting very old. But then the cards would be thrown away, usually when someone noticed they were gathering dust. And no one would mention the mysterious Aunt Gee Gee again for awhile.

Until the day Aunt Gee Gee called Jack's home and insisted on seeing her dear nephew.

Jack stepped inside and blinked several times to get used to the light. He started to smile — then he stopped.

This was all wrong. His brain stalled, unable to take in this new information. His aunt wasn't ancient. She didn't smell of old lady lavender.

She was ghoulishly young.

Jack had thought she would look like his mom — plump and comfortably reassuring. Though of course much, much older. But Gee Gee was neither. Tall and thin, she had deathly white skin with no hint of color. A frizzy ripple of fiery red hair fell down her back, all the way to her knees. She wore a moth-eaten black ball gown, filthy combat boots, and a battered top hat that was covered in a thick layer of dust. Jack realized this was why her head had seemed so long.

Then he shook himself as he worked out the amazing truth. *Wow, she's had a load of plastic surgery,* he thought. *She must be rich!*

That would explain why her eyes were so strange — yellow with slit pupils, just like a snake. Jack was impressed. He'd never seen anyone with contact lenses like that before. He stared in fascination.

Then he grinned as he started to think about all the things he could buy, thanks to a rich relative handing him cash for birthdays and Christmas. *I have to make sure she likes me,* he thought.

Jack took a big breath and for some reason began to stammer, something he only did when he was very nervous. "H-h-hello, A-aunty!"

She beamed in reply and ushered him all the way through the door. It slammed — *BANG* — at his back and made him jump.

"Well, Jackie-poo," she drawled, "I suppose you'll be wanting your supper!" She smiled, showing a row of perfect white teeth that were ever so slightly sharp. "Just make yourself comfortable while I go and dish it up."

She shoved him toward an open door that led to the living room, then wandered off down the hall humming something that sounded strangely like "Jingle Bells."

Jack ducked under the doorframe (the house had obviously been made for the real seven dwarfs). Looking around, he caught his breath in wonder. Cats. They were everywhere. Big fat glossy ones, skinny scrawny spitting ones, fighting and yowling over the best place to lie next to a roaring fire.

They all fell silent when Jack walked in, and they stared at him with narrowed eyes.

One bony cat deliberately chewed a piece of raw fish, making a *SHULURP, SHULURP, SHULUUUUURP* noise.

Jack scowled. He hated cats.

Just then his aunt walked in, so he pasted a beaming smile on his face.

"Now, now, kitties," she said, "this is Jack, my great-great, er, *greatest-ever* nephew, and we're all going to be SUPER nice to him while he stays with us." Her expression suddenly changed from sweet to terrifying and her face contorted into a snarl. "AREN'T WE?" she thundered.

But the cats seemed unimpressed. They just carried on fighting.

Jack raised his eyebrows. With that booming voice, he wondered if Aunt Gee Gee had earned all her money from being an actress. Jack decided she must be really lonely to need so many cats. He felt a bit sorry for her. A rich old lady with lots of cats.

Aunt Gee Gee walked through the room, sending the cats scampering like Skittles out of the way, then sat down in a rocking chair. She gestured for Jack to sit down too. He gingerly picked his way through the carpet of cats and perched on the edge of the sofa, trying to ignore the dozens of eyes that glared at him from the floor.

His aunt smiled and handed him a steaming plate of food which had been sitting next to her chair under a tarnished silver cover. Jack took the dish gratefully. He was actually quite hungry. Until he glanced at it. On the plate was a swollen black mass of jelly. He recoiled in disgust.

"Pickled pig's heart, dearie. The best for miles around!" She beamed. "Come on, you can't let it go to waste. Eat up!"

Jack smiled weakly and picked up his fork. He poked the food and the whole thing quivered. He thought he was going to vomit all over the cats.

Still, he cut off a shivering piece of the runny goo and put it in his mouth. Being the smallest in his grade — well, the whole school — meant he was used to doing stupid dares to prove how tough he was. He chewed carefully, wrinkling his nose. The heart had no taste and just slid unpleasantly round his mouth, sticky and thick. But he lifted his head and forced a weak smile. "Um. Yummy!" he spluttered.

Aunt Gee Gee grinned so widely, Jack could see all her teeth again. He thought uncomfortably that it made her look like a wolf eyeing up its dinner.

"That's a good boy," she crooned and settled back into the huge overstuffed armchair opposite him. It sent out billows of dust as she did. "There's nothing like it for growing children. So, I've prepared a room for you in the attic. It's a little, er, bare, but I'm sure you won't mind that, will you?"

Jack shook his head, and while she turned away to pick up one of the cats, he quietly spat out the pig's heart and fed it to a tabby beside him. His aunt's head snapped around.

Jack gave a faint smile. He realized with a feeling of dread that he would have to eat the rest of his revolting supper after all.

* * *

After his dinner (which involved Jack chewing in painful silence and his aunt staring at him with a wide grin the entire time), Aunt Gee Gee led the way up the narrow wooden staircase. Carelessly, she walked through the thick cobwebs that hung from the ceiling as they climbed the creaking wooden stairs. They clung to Jack's face and made him choke. *Honestly,* he thought, *someone so rich should be able to afford help cleaning the place!* Come to think of it, he hadn't seen any TVs. Or computers. He paled. A whole holiday with no internet access or TV . . . ?

Jack thought longingly of his warm room at home. Of his favorite mashed potatoes. He wondered if having pots of money to spend on new stuff was really worth visiting this place and decided, reluctantly, it probably wasn't.

"Now, Jackie-poo," his aunt trilled, ignoring Jack's venomous expression at the nickname. "I have to pop along to, er, bingo tonight with some of my girlfriends. *So* sorry to do this to you on your first night. I'll be back just after midnight."

Jack could have sworn she was being secretive. Before he had time to dwell on that, Aunt Gee Gee screeched to a halt in front of a bolted wooden door. Jack gasped. There were two intertwined, hissing snakes carved into it. They were slowly moving in a writhing circle.

"Cool!" he breathed. "How'd you do that? Is it a hologram or something?"

Aunt Gee Gee gave a little laugh, said something about the wonders of electrical gadgets these days, and threw open the door. It slammed into the wall, and mounds of centuries-old dust fell across Jack's first view of the room.

Coughing, and perhaps swearing, he peered through the gloom. The light from Aunt Gee Gee's candle struggled through the coarse shadows. The room was tiny and bare, except for a small wooden table next to the bed, which sat under a grimy window. Aunt Gee Gee bustled into the room, beckoning for Jack to follow her.

"Now," she said briskly. "You've been fed and watered, so be a good child and go to sleep. I expect you're awfully tired, dearie."

This was obviously not a question, so Jack just nodded.

"Jolly good! Well, you put your head down and get a good night's sleep." She swung around to leave and then gave another silly little laugh. "Oops, I nearly forgot to leave you a candle — how naughty of me!"

Jack, who had been watching her retreating back with slight horror, felt relieved at the reappearance of the candle. The tiny flickering light seemed his only friend. The cats didn't seem the cuddly kind, even if he had been a cat person. They had been creeping up from downstairs and littered the wooden steps. A brave few were sitting at Aunt Gee Gee's feet, watching Jack with hostile eyes.

Sitting glumly on the bed, he held out his hand for the candle. Aunt Gee Gee seemed to recoil for a moment and her nose scrunched up in disgust. Jack was bewildered. It almost felt as if she couldn't bear to go near him. Like he smelled funny.

Jack dropped his hand and swallowed.

Aunt Gee Gee blinked her strange, yellow eyes and carefully laid the candle on his bedside table. She gave a small sigh of relief and swung around once more to leave.

Then he watched her back stiffen. She slowly turned to face him. Her face was blank and when she spoke, her lips did not move. Instead, a deep, distorted voice boomed around the room. "You will not, under any condition, go into the forest when I am gone. There are untold dangers there that will turn your hair white and leave you screaming every night for the rest of your life."

Jack paled. He would have cried out, but Aunt Gee Gee suddenly blinked. Her face smoothed, and she looked as she had before she had spoken in that unsettling voice.

"Well, cheerio, dearie!" she cooed. "I'll give your mom a ring to let her know you have arrived safely — for now." She gave a sharp-toothed grin, blew a kiss at him, and whirled out of the door, which slammed closed.

Jack released the breath he hadn't known he was holding and gave a shaky laugh. "Freaky skills," he muttered to himself. He wondered if all the plastic surgery had done something to her vocal cords. Maybe that explained the scary voice. Her face was probably always getting stuck due to all the surgery.

Jack paused as a strange feeling trickled over him. He looked up and let out a strangled yell as he saw two enormous, luminous eyes gazing down at him.

CHAPTER 3

THE TREE GUARDIAN

The cat ran yowling to the door, where it miraculously stretched itself flat and scampered under the frame. It didn't want to stay after being shouted at. It wanted to return to the comfort of the fire and relief from odd human children.

Jack groaned and lay back on the bed for a few minutes of peace. "Just a cat. It was just . . . a . . . cat," he said firmly. He kept repeating it to himself until he felt calmer. This was short-lived however, because the room was drafty, and a cold wind curled around him. He sat up, shivering.

He turned and wiped the dirt from the tiny window next to the bed and squinted at the forest outside. It was immense. The trees writhed and stretched toward the dark sky, which wasn't as black as the shadows he could see beneath the skeletal branches. A lone owl soared above the treetops before swooping into the spiraling darkness, targeting some unseen prey.

Jack sat this way for several minutes, watching the rippling of the trees as the wind threaded its way through the forest. The minutes ticked by, as slow as mold climbing a wall.

If he were at home, Jack thought, he would be curled up in front of the TV, watching his favorite program next to the fire and sipping hot chocolate. His mom would be tapping away on her phone and his dad snoozing in his chair. The dog would be happily panting at his feet and letting a pool of saliva drip on the carpet. He would not be gradually turning into a human icicle and shooing away scary, mangy, flea-ridden cats.

A moan from the forest drew his attention as a particularly strong gust of wind made an ancient oak creak.

He started to feel curious.

Jack began to wonder what it would be like to have a peek, just a tiny peek, at the forest. He gazed out of the dirty window. Suddenly, he saw a hooded, hunched figure scurry down the dirt path that led from the cottage garden to the forest. The figure was carrying a large bag, bulging with rectangular bundles. Jack frowned. He tried to remember where he had seen something like that before. Then he realized where — it was in a movie about a bank robbery. The rectangular bundles looked like stacks of money.

The figure turned around, and a blurry face framed with red hair peered back at the house. Realizing who it was, Jack sat up quickly and pressed his nose flat against the window before pulling away and furiously wiping a sleeve over the dirty glass. Then he thrust his nose back against the window . . . just in time to see his aunt disappear into the mist of the forest.

Jack sat back with a triumphant grin. *No one plays bingo in the middle of the night in the deserted countryside. She's up to something,* he thought. He bit his lip, something he did when concentrating. *She's carrying a load of money around. Maybe she doesn't trust banks and hides her money in the forest.*

Now, if Jack had been a sensible boy or at least a little more intelligent, he would have wrapped himself in the moldy old blanket, prayed for morning to arrive, and gone to sleep.

As it was, he forgot that curiosity had killed the cat (and ignored the fact that the cats were snoozing safely inside the house). He jumped off the bed, stuffed his feet into his shoes, grabbed his jacket, and ran down the stairs two at a time. Then he was through the front door, walking down the path, and disappearing into the same mist as his mysterious aunt.

* * *

Jack wandered along the mossy ground and ducked under the tree branches that tried to whip his face. The clouds had blown away to reveal a full moon, so he had a little light to navigate the path. In the distance he could just see the hunched figure of his aunt. She had pulled up the hood of her velvet cloak, and her shadow was dark on the ground, cutting through the moonlight.

As Jack trudged through the dead leaves, he tried to ignore the growing uneasiness he felt.

Finally his aunt slowed and came to a halt in front of a large oak tree covered in moss. Jack dropped to his knees in the mud. She glanced over her shoulder then lifted her hand and knocked firmly on the tree three times.

Jack watched in astonishment as part of the trunk creaked open like a door. His aunt disappeared inside the tree trunk.

He stood up and stared. Was this where she stashed the money? Jack waited for her to come out, but nothing happened. His fingers started to go numb from the cold, and all he could hear was the hooting of a nearby owl.

Jack had a sudden vision of his aunt being stuck inside the tree. Was there any oxygen in there? With a gasp he rushed toward the tree. He skidded to a halt in front of the massive trunk, gnarled with age.

Telling himself how surprised his aunt would be when he opened the door and saved her (she might even give him a nice cash reward), Jack banged on the tree trunk.

"I know you're in there!" he shouted. "I'll get you out, don't worry! Aunt Gee Gee? Hellooo?"

Silence.

Jack tried to find the edge of the door to pull it open. He ran his hands down the rough bark but couldn't feel an edge. He punched the tree three times in frustration, then winced, cradling his hurt hand. *Hitting stuff actually hurts,* he thought in bewilderment. *They make it look so easy in the movies.*

Then a door made of moss and bark slowly swung open.

Jack jumped backward with a cry. He stared down at his

hands. *I hit it three times and it opened,* he thought, *just like my aunt did.* He frowned and shook his head. *Just coincidence. I must've dislodged the dirt or something.*

Thrusting his chin in the air, Jack stepped inside. To his amazement, he discovered that the tree was a lot bigger inside than he had thought. It felt like a large and dim room. "I'm here. I'll save you!" he shouted into the gloom.

Then a high-pitched voice piped back, "That will be one dream, please, master."

Jack looked wildly around for the voice and found he was staring at the strangest person he had ever seen in his life — a man no more than two feet tall, with orange tufts of hair and a pair of tusks growing out of his forehead. His face seemed like a man's — but was made entirely of sagging wrinkles, like a walnut. And he was glaring at Jack.

Jack stepped back. *Wow. OK,* he thought, *Aunt Gee Gee just has some seriously eccentric friends. Maybe he's trying to look like a famous movie character or something?* Jack eyed the man up and down to try to find something that made sense. He shook his head in confusion. He couldn't think of any character who looked like this.

The man was sitting on the floor and had a huge metal chain wrapped round one ankle, which was tied to a tree root. He rattled the chain and scowled. "I said, that will be one dream, please! What's wrong? What are you staring at?"

Jack felt irritated that this person was looking at him as though *he* was the one behaving strangely — as if it was perfectly normal to be sitting in a tree in the middle of the night.

"Hang on, where's my aunt? What do you mean 'one dream' and, well, what're you doing here anyway? And why are you chained to the inside of a tree?" Jack's voice rose hysterically, and he had to take a deep breath to calm himself. *OK*, he thought. *No way that face is real; it must be make-up or something. I'm in the middle of a prank video, and my aunt is in on it. Any second now, someone will jump out with a camera and yell, "Gotcha!"*

The man raised one orange bushy eyebrow, which was lost in his wrinkled face. Jack found himself fascinated by the tusks stuck on the man's forehead. *How did he make those?* Jack thought. He could see every part of the tusks in detail, even down to the slight cracks in them — from age, perhaps?

Jack felt a sudden needle of fear shoot through his stomach. He pushed it down angrily. "You're so short!" he blurted out.

"How rude. Children these days have no respect!" the man squeaked. "When I was a young'un, three thousand years ago, mind, I spoke politely to my elders or they would have boiled me in oil and fed me to a warthog! And I'll have you know that you're not much taller yourself, despite being one of those great, lumbering humans! Perhaps you were switched at birth with one of my kind, hmm?" Seeing Jack's bewildered face, he sighed. "I'm a goblin, you foolish boy!"

Jack gave a little laugh, which sounded forced even to him. "Yeah, right, a goblin. This is just a prank. One massive joke by my batty aunt. She's going to put a recording of this online, and people all over the world will laugh at me. Nice one."

"All right, laddie, I can tell you're not the sharpest twig in the forest, so I'll fill you in on some facts of life." Gesturing grandly, the man continued, "I am the goblin guardian of this doorway and, as this is the Dreamer's Tree, you have to pay me one dream to pass. If you have no imagination and are as dumb as you look, then you can't pass. It's that simple, dung brains."

Jack turned an interesting shade of brilliant red. "Stop it, just stop it!" he spat. "I don't know why you're doing this, but I know it's a prank, right?"

The man stayed silent. He drummed his nails on the chain, making a clinking noise. Jack noticed that his nails had been made to look like long, wickedly sharp black claws. For some reason, this made Jack even more furious.

"Fine! You want me to play along? OK, as my aunt's made such a big effort to make me look like an idiot, I'll play along with your game. You want to know a dream? I dream that I will wake up, in my bed, and find this is all a nightmare and I never had to visit this place! I dream I'll wake up and have . . . Coco Pops for breakfast, and then play for *hours* on my computer!" He paused to catch his breath, then leaned forward into the little man's astonished face. "I'll watch TV for the rest of the day and never have to think about trees, forests or — or — or goblin keeper thingies EVER AGAIN!" Jack shouted, spraying the man with spittle.

Calmly, the man pulled a large spotted handkerchief from the pocket of his worn breeches and wiped his face. He stood up and said in amazement, "Well, laddie, that would be the strangest dream I've heard in a long time! How MARVELOUS!"

Jack's mouth fell open in amazement.

"What talk of pops made out of cocoa, and com-pu-ters!" he said with wonderment. "You may be a puny excuse of a human, but, well, wowzarooney!" The man drew himself up to his full two-foot height and said with pride, "You may enter, oh bard of the forest! Enter and behold the wonders of the glade."

Jack was about to ask what he was babbling on about when he noticed a light shining behind the man's head. There was another door on the far side of the tree. And it was opening.

"OK," Jack said, "is that where the cameras are? And I guess there are microphones above me." He glanced up. "I get it — ha, ha, very funny. Can we stop now so I can go back before I freeze to death?"

The second doorway creaked fully open, letting in the light and spilling dust and insects on the floor. There was a large forest outside the door. It wasn't the same place Jack had just left.

"That's impossible," murmured Jack. He forgot his

confusion and stepped past the giggling man into the misty light, putting one trembling foot outside the door. "Feels solid." With a gulp, he poked his head out. It was definitely a different forest. The trees were huge, twice the size of the ones he had walked past on the way here. The moon shone brightly, but there was something odd about it. Jack blanched. The moon was a sickly blue, not white.

For the first time, Jack let himself wonder if he had stumbled into something bigger than he could ever have imagined. He scrutinized the little man behind him, who stared back with bright eyes. *Goblin*, Jack thought in wonder.

Then he shook his head. Stuff like that was for kids. It didn't exist. Not in the real world. But he was going to find out just how crazy — and hopefully, just how rich — his aunt really was. If she'd built a gigantic movie set just for her own fun, well, then she was richer than he'd thought. He took a deep breath and stepped out into the woods. The door creaked shut behind him, sealing his fate.

CHAPTER 4

THE CAROUSEL CAULDRON

Jack tried to pretend he wasn't afraid as he walked into the strange new forest. The air was as silent as a graveyard. The branches of the trees were motionless, and no animals broke the eerie silence of the night. He walked on, determined to solve the mystery of his aunt.

Despite telling himself over and over that there was no such thing, a small part of Jack started to feel as though he had fallen into a fairy tale. He remembered what happened to people in stories who refused to believe their own eyes. He had the uncomfortable feeling they came to a sticky end. His history teacher, Professor Footnote, always droned on about the "happily ever after" myth and how, in real fairy tales, people were usually skinned alive, or something equally nasty. Jack had listened, fascinated, even though half the class was busy texting under their desks. Jack really liked history. His dad said it was a waste of time.

Jack saw a brightly lit blob on the horizon and he trotted eagerly toward it, hoping it was perhaps a supermarket. Then, if this really was just a big prank, he could call his parents and get them to drive over and pick him up while he waited in the brightly lit security of the candy aisle.

As the blob grew more solid, Jack slowed his pace and stared. Nothing, not even a tree that was really a doorway, a magical aunt, or a two-foot prisoner goblin, could have prepared him for the thing in the moonlit glade.

An old-fashioned carousel spun in the center of the grass. It appeared to be abandoned — as if it had been standing there for hundreds of years. The tarnished wooden horses rolled around on their endless journey, staring with open mouths and sightless eyes. The carousel's crimson and gold paint had long ago started to peel and fade. Dark shadows danced around the horses.

Now he could hear eerie organ music floating through the night air.

Ba-ba da-ba DUM DUM DUM, ba-ba da-ba DUM DUM DUM.

The carousel creaked as it revolved to the music. Then Jack realized that what he had thought were dark shadows were actually figures sitting on the painted horses.

Women dressed like his aunt, in top hats and flowing gowns, sat sidesaddle on the horses. Their skirts swirled around their combat boots as the horses dipped and turned on their endless gallop. The women laughed and hummed along to the music, showing flashing teeth and glimmering eyes. Like his aunt, they were all bloodlessly pale.

He saw at the base of the carousel the bag Aunt Gee Gee had been carrying. The contents spilled out. *Just rectangular lumps of firewood,* he thought, feeling foolish. There had been no money after all.

Jack watched as the women all reached up and removed their top hats. Then he gasped in horror when he saw what the hats were hiding.

A scrawny neck grew on top of each woman's head! The thin necks supported shrunken, mummified heads, wrapped in filthy brown bandages that fluttered in the breeze. Jack caught glimpses of the heads' ancient, empty eyes. He fell to his knees and clamped his hands over his mouth, trying not to scream, but the image was so horrible he had to cram his fist into his mouth and bite down on his knuckles.

The women all sighed with relief at having taken off their hats, then started to cackle with glee. The mummified heads grinned.

Jack scrambled to his feet and began to back away as the full meaning of the scene hit him. Wisps of smoke rose from the top of the carousel, where a foul mixture bubbled and spat over the edges of the roof. The wooden horses below worked as enormous spoons that leisurely stirred the mixture inside the hollow carousel. It was a giant's mixing bowl — and, in all the old fairy tales Jack had read, there was only one thing that giants liked to eat. Children.

Was *he* meant to go in the pot?

That small nagging voice inside Jack — which had been growing louder as he walked through the forest — suddenly began to shout. *It's real, it's real, oh God, it's real!*

All his bravado fell away, and Jack realized the truth. He was in danger.

At that moment, the carousel started to spin faster. Round and round it went until the women and the horses were a blur of color. The women's laughter became more high-pitched until a terrible screeching filled the air.

Then he saw his Aunt Gee Gee, holding a long stick over her head. It looked like a curved horn made of black ivory. She pointed it at the sky. There was a rolling rumble of thunder and then lightning cracked through the air. Jack looked up, but there were no storm clouds. Where was the lightning coming from?

Over and over it flashed, striking the center of the carousel each time.

The women started to chant in a low, rough language Jack didn't recognize. The carousel began to slow as their chanting grew louder.

"Doth, loch, lach vianta, doth loch lach VIANTA!" they chanted.

Jack stared in mute horror as thick green smoke poured from the top of the carousel.

The chanting was deafening now, the women almost screaming the words.

"DOTH, LOCH, LACH VIANTA, DOTH LOCH LACH VIANTA!"

Jack shrank backward and accidentally put his foot on a dry twig, which made a tiny snapping sound.

The chanting stopped instantly.

Jack held his breath. *There's no way they could've heard me,* he thought.

But the women flicked their heads to the side and sniffed the air, making wet, sucking sounds. Their second heads bared needle sharp teeth.

"I smell human child," hissed a dark-haired woman. They all peered into the darkness, sniffing and searching.

Aunt Gee Gee jumped off the carousel. "That's not possible. No brat has ever set foot in the Lost Forest. They would never dare!"

Jack tried to stand up, but staggered and fell over again. His legs wouldn't seem to obey his mind.

The dark-haired woman scowled. "Then let's make sure, sister. Release the tortured souls from the cauldron. They can search for any meddling humans!"

The women muttered their agreement.

Aunt Gee Gee rolled her eyes. "Fine! But you've been *so* paranoid since those vampire hunters tried to stake you three hundred years ago!"

"I'm not paranoid! It took me decades to grow another heart and I've *still* got the scars!"

With an impatient sigh, Aunt Gee Gee rolled up her

sleeves. She threw back her head and cried, "Come to me, all those souls who fell prey to the spells spun by my dark sisters! Rise and find the foolish child who dares enter our lair."

Helplessly, Jack watched as the women joined hands and closed their eyes. The green smoke began to thicken and rise. It stank of sulfur and floated in his direction. Horribly, there seemed to be writhing shapes in it. Jack tried to make out the hunched shapes in the mist, but they constantly shifted and morphed.

Stand UP, Jack, he thought furiously, willing his legs to carry him. With an almighty effort, he wrenched himself to his feet and backed away from the evil mist, but it was too late. It had drifted away from the cauldron and was heading right for him. To his horror, he could see hundreds of blood-red eyes gleaming in the smoke, and he knew something was looking for intruders. For him.

Jack started to panic. His breath grew short, and he felt as though he was suffocating. Gasping, he doubled over. Then he felt a sharp nip on his ankle. Jumping a foot in the air, he screeched, "Ow!" and landed with a thump. Terrified, Jack saw a pair of feline blue eyes. A silky cat was sitting next to him, its fur the color of pure white milk. With a dainty tug, the cat fastened its teeth onto his trouser leg and pulled. He stared at the cat in fear, hoping it wasn't another freaky creature. The cat's intention, though, was obvious. It wanted him to leave the glade.

"Yep," Jack whispered, "got it! See ya."

On shaky legs, Jack turned to leave. But the cat jumped onto his leg, then ran up to his shoulder, where it clung on.

Jack gave a muffled cry. "What're you doing? Get off! I hate cats!" He swatted at the cat, but it didn't seem to want to let go. Desperately, Jack turned in small circles, trying to push the animal off his shoulder. Then it gave a meow of warning. Jack looked up. The green mist was only a few feet away. Suddenly, his small passenger was the least of his worries.

Swearing, Jack gathered his courage and turned his back on the cloud, then began to run back the way he had come.

"Fine," he hissed at the cat. "But don't blame me if you fall off and break your neck!"

The cat gave a smug meow and tightened its grip on his sweater.

Jack ran for his life.

But the mist from the weird potion floated on the wind faster than Jack could run. Tiny tendrils slithered in front of his eyes, temporarily blinding him. It poured down his throat and up his nose. He coughed and spluttered, feeling his lungs burning up. Low branches whipped his face, and he jumped the fallen logs in his path. The cat clung on stubbornly.

Nearing exhaustion, Jack looked over his shoulder. The rest of the mist was gaining on him. He just couldn't outrun it. Chest heaving, he fell with a crash. He tried to get up, but his legs were shaking too badly. Waves of black blurred his vision as faintness stole over him. He fought to stay conscious. He could see the hideous shapes moving through the smoke and knew he was about to be swallowed up by them. He was done for. Jack closed his eyes tightly and rested his head on the grass. He clenched his fists and moaned, waiting for the mist to take him.

But instead he felt a stinging pain on his hand.

"Ouch!" he cried, opening his eyes. The white cat had scuttled down from his shoulder and scratched his hand. Blood dripped from four deep wounds. Astonished, he watched as the cat raised one paw and prepared to swipe again.

"Stop that!" he said. "Isn't it bad enough that I'm going to die? You don't have to torture me too!"

The cat paused and made a sound that was almost a grunt of disdain. Then, very deliberately, it scratched him again.

"Ow!" Jack cried. The pain was electric and made him stagger to his feet, cradling his hurt hand. "What did you do that for, you mangy —"

He looked down at his feet and gaped. "Oh! I can stand!"

The cat meowed and ran up his shoulder. Then it put out one paw, clearly meaning to swipe at his face with its sharp claws.

Jack took the hint and started to run.

The mist was only inches away, but Jack refused to look back. He ran faster than he had ever moved in his life, leaping over the branches that littered the forest floor, knowing that one more fall would mean his doom.

Finally, after a long, blind race through the growing fog, he dimly saw the outline of the tree that led back to his world.

The cat meowed and Jack said, "Yeah, I see it! I see it!"

He almost sobbed with relief as he raced to the door. He banged on the door three times, then grasped the edges and pulled, tearing his fingernails. He stumbled through the doorway and slammed the door behind him. The mist was locked on the other side and didn't follow him into the tree. Jack leaned his head against the rough bark and let out a shaky sigh. He was safe.

The cat meowed again. Jack swallowed hard. "Sorry I tried to, you know, chuck you off back there," he said. "I'm pretty sure you just saved my life. So, um, yeah — thanks."

Jack hesitated, then reached up and ran one hand over the cat's soft head. The cat purred in his ear. Jack smiled. He turned round, preparing to leave. But then he saw a dark shape move and jumped. The man — *no*, he thought, *the goblin* — was lying on the floor. He was asleep and snoring like a jackhammer.

The goblin chuckled between snores and whispered something that sounded like "Coco Popsssss . . ."

Jack was fascinated by what he now believed to be a real live goblin. But he decided it was more important to leave. He cared more about his own skin than the realization that everything he thought he knew about the world was wrong. He wasn't safe, and he had to leave quickly.

Jack grabbed the door handle to his own world and pulled. The golden light of dawn lit his face as the door creaked open.

Behind him, the goblin stirred and whispered to his

retreating back, "Well then, looks like you escaped the witch and her cronies. But I don't think she'll let you go again, oh bard."

Jack froze. Without turning round, he said, "She didn't let me go. She just didn't see me. She didn't know I was there." He slipped through the door, with the cat curled up on his shoulder.

In the darkness of the tree, the goblin laughed quietly. "That's what they *all* say, dearie. And they're *all* long dead."

* * *

Jack made his way back to the house. He was exhausted, battered, bruised, frightened witless — and he had a new pet. He pulled himself up the winding stairs to his room. The white cat meowed, jumped to the floor, and ran round his feet while he clattered into his drafty bedroom. Jack wasn't sure what to make of the creature. The world he had found it in was definitely not normal.

He frowned. "So," he said, "are you a he or a she?" For some reason, he had a feeling the cat was a girl. When she curled up around his feet like a delightful hot water bottle, warming his numb toes, Jack wondered what to call her. "Don't suppose you can speak, can you cat?" he mumbled, half asleep. "I don't have the foggiest idea what to call you . . ." As he trailed off into the land of dreams, a whisper reached his ears, in the moment between waking and dreaming. He could have sworn he heard someone purr a name, something like "Rrrrreal," but then it was gone and he was safely in a dream.

CHAPTER 5

ESCAPE

Jack woke up in the morning with a splitting headache. His hands and face looked as if they had been dragged through dank soil. His hair also stuck up in five directions. He realized his legs were stiff and aching. He groaned in pain.

Looking down at the bottom of the bed, he saw the white cat contentedly washing her frosted fur with a very pink tongue. When she noticed he was awake, she gave a yowl and sprang onto his shoulder. She curled around his neck like a warm scarf and began to purr.

Jack was about to chuck her off, but he hesitated, then shrugged instead. Although he still hated cats, this one seemed to be growing on him. Unfortunately the feeling soon passed when he remembered why she was there. And where he was. And what had happened.

Terror hit him hard in the stomach.

"Arrrrrgggggghhhhh!" he shouted, falling out of bed and

onto the floor with a thud. The cat jumped off his neck with an indignant hiss.

Breathing hard, he grasped his throat, remembering the feeling of the mist rolling into his lungs. Had it been real? Maybe he'd just dreamed it. Maybe he'd passed out in the tree trunk after getting stuck inside, and his oxygen-deprived brain had made it all up. That would explain the feeling of choking.

Jack sighed with relief. *Of course, that's what happened — I just dreamed it,* he thought. Feeling much better, he stretched and pulled on the sweater he'd dumped on the floor last night. It was hard with dried mud. He frowned and shook his head. "Must've fallen over on the way back," he muttered.

He thrust his hands through the armholes and saw that his nails were grimy. Jack shrugged — there was nothing unusual about that.

He opened the bedroom door and picked up the cat, who he decided was just a stray who had followed him back to the house, then started down the rickety staircase to face his aunt.

When Jack came to the bottom of the stairs, he saw that billows of steam were pouring from the cracks in the kitchen doorframe. Jack had a moment of terror, remembering the mist from the night before. (*Just a dream,* he reminded himself. *Just. A. Dream.*) To Jack's relief this seemed like normal steam.

"JACKIE-POO!" someone screeched from the kitchen.

"Well, no prizes for guessing who that is," Jack murmured to the white cat. She wriggled and jumped to the floor, hiding under a nearby chair. But Jack wasn't as confident as he sounded. Deep down, he was thinking about what the goblin (*eccentric local,* he insisted furiously) had said.

That his aunt was a dangerous witch.

Jack remembered from all the old fairy tales what happened to children who came across witches. They were cooked and eaten.

Jack swallowed hard and stepped into the kitchen. He fixed his best smile on his face. The steam blinded him for a moment. Then he made out the figure of his aunt standing next to a large black bubbling pot. She wore a long flowery apron over her ball gown, her top hat, and a pair of enormous pink oven gloves. She stirred the contents of the pot and pushed down something that seemed to be trying to crawl out of one side.

Retreating, Jack promptly tripped over several mangy cats and had to resist the urge to kick them through the window.

Aunt Gee Gee fixed her weird yellow eyes on him. "Well, how are we this morning, young Jackie? Sleep well?"

Jack suppressed a snort of hysterical laughter and replied, "Er, well enough. Nice room! Very, um, healthy, you know — it's good for the back to have a hard mattress."

She stared at him. Then she deliberately lifted the wooden spoon she was holding. Jack began to panic, thinking she was going to hit him with it, then drag him screaming into the boiling pot. To his relief, she turned toward the pot and waved away the billows of steam. She reached in with the spoon and slopped a mass of water and fur onto a plate.

Jack nearly gasped with relief, but it was short-lived.

He wondered where she had learned to cook. The sewer seemed quite likely.

He would have said the thing floating in the watery grease was a rat. But it had no head or tail, and it was perfectly round.

Jack put the plate down on the kitchen table when his aunt's back was turned. As he expected, a skinny cat with one eye sprang up on the table and snatched the food from the plate. The cat then fell off the table head first, dragged down by the weight of the mysterious food. It hit the floor like a cannonball.

Aunt Gee Gee snapped back round at the noise, but Jack just smiled and pointed at the empty plate.

She raised her eyebrows and said, "My goodness, you're a hungry boy, aren't you? Yes you are!"

"Yummmm," Jack replied, pretending to be savoring a piece of food stuck in his teeth. *Well,* he thought, *it looks chewy enough.*

"I know that you will want to leave me today to return home . . . ," Aunt Gee Gee began.

"No!" Jack tried to protest, while pretending it wasn't a blatant lie — and that there was food still stuck in his teeth. This proved to be too much for his acting ability. He just looked as though he needed the toilet.

Aunt Gee Gee laughed, making a sound like breaking glass.

"Oh Jackie-poo, I know you so well already. I know you'll want to go home." Placing one finger on her chin, she said, "But I just CAN'T UNDERSTAND why you do."

Jack felt a trickle of sweat drip down his back. *Don't freak out,* he thought. *There's no way she knows I followed her. She's not a witch, but she still might be angry that I didn't stay in the house like she told me to.*

His aunt moved away from the cauldron and opened a tall cupboard in the corner of the kitchen. Brass pots and pans hung from the top of the cupboard, and they clanged together as she pushed them out of the way. Finally she pulled out a chipped pot with a round lid.

"Aha!" she said triumphantly. "I knew this was still, well, HIDING around here somewhere!" She turned and dumped the pot on the kitchen table in front of Jack.

The white cat, who had been sitting quietly under the chair all this time, let out a hiss and leaped onto the table. She curled up around the pot and snarled at Aunt Gee Gee.

Jack blinked with surprise. He'd never heard a cat snarl before.

Aunt Gee Gee's face turned first gray, then brilliant pink.

"GET THAT UNNATURAL THING OFF MY TABLE!" she roared.

Hurriedly, Jack reached forward and scooped the cat up in his arms. But the cat had suddenly become demented. She writhed and hissed. Her flying claws and fangs made Jack drop her, and she sped out of the kitchen door.

Aunt Gee Gee let out a frustrated scream, threw back her head, and shouted, "GET THAT CURSED CAT! GET HER BEFORE SHE ESCAPES AGAIN!"

Escapes? Jack thought. Then, to his horror, the other cats in the house all ran after her, as smoothly and suddenly as a flock of geese turning in the sky.

Jack watched helplessly as the last cat raced out the kitchen door. Aunt Gee Gee stood rigid with anger for a moment — and Jack remembered what he'd dreamed was under her top hat. He could have sworn the hat teetered on her head, as though its occupant was squirming to get out. But then Aunt Gee Gee twirled on the tips of her toes and faced Jack, her face eerily calm. The hat became still once more. Jack gulped hard. *There's nothing there,* he thought. *Honestly, nothing is under her hat. It's. Just. A. Hat.*

"Well," she said. "I don't know how that *awful* creature got into the house and I don't know *how* she got here from —" Aunt Gee stopped speaking. "But we won't dwell on that, shall we? And just as I was going to give you your farewell present too!" She pouted and tapped one of her long fingernails on the lid of the pot. Jack eyed it closely and realized four words were written in a flowing, faded script on the side. They said *Ye Olde Cookie Jar.*

Aunt Gee Gee followed his gaze and said, "Oh, aren't you a clever boy! You can read! I didn't realize children were so well educated these days."

Jack scowled.

"I want to give you a little something, to remind you of your time here. But you must never, ever open it."

Aunt Gee Gee smiled at Jack's confused face. "You must never open the lid and eat the delicious, scrumptious cookies inside. They are the most sensational cookies known to this world. I baked them myself."

At this point she tried to blush modestly but couldn't quite pull it off.

"They are warm and fresh and gooey inside. They smell like a birthday cake lifted straight from the oven."

Jack felt his mouth water at the thought of chocolate chunks melting into warm, sweet cookie dough. The idea of breaking one in half and sinking his teeth into it made him want to rip the lid off the jar. His eyes glazed over with visions of sugar . . . then he saw Aunt Gee Gee's face.

She was watching him eagerly, her eyes narrowed, a nasty smirk on her pale lips. Jack remembered the plates of goo she had tried to feed him. The smile faded from his face. He thought the cookie jar might contain a couple of rotten pig's feet soaking in their own blood, or something else equally vile.

As soon as Jack got out of there, he was going to heave the jar off the nearest cliff.

His aunt handed him the cookie jar. It was heavier than he expected and a lot bigger. He couldn't see over the top of the jar when he held it. It was cracked all over with black lines and creamy colored with age.

Briskly, his aunt said, "Now that's over with, off you pop. Go on. Shoo."

For a second, Jack thought she must be talking to one of the cats. But she was looking right at him. She turned and walked along the hall to the front door. Standing by the door, she beckoned to Jack. Bewildered, Jack walked over. "Um, Aunt Gee Gee, I haven't packed or anyth— Oh."

His suitcase was standing by the door.

Grasping the jar with one hand, Jack hesitantly picked up his suitcase with the other, juggling the two.

Without smiling, Aunt Gee Gee opened the front door. The rusty hinges squealed in protest. She cocked her head to one side, staring at Jack the way a cat looks at a bird . . . then she pushed him through the door and — *BANG* — slammed it shut behind him.

It was pouring rain. Jack stood in a huge puddle of muddy water. But he didn't care. He'd had enough of his batty aunt and couldn't wait to get back to normality.

Just then, Jack became aware of the enticing aroma of freshly baked cookies. He slowly looked down at the pot in his arms.

The cookie jar smelled delicious.

CHAPTER 6

HOME SWEET HOME?

Four hours later, Jack stood outside his parents' house, clutching his suitcase, a hyperactive cat, and the cookie jar. He was attracting a lot of funny looks from his neighbors, who peered out at him from behind twitching curtains.

The white cat had been waiting for him at the train station, looking wind-blown but alive. She had sprung onto his shoulder with a yowl and remained there for the journey home, purring into his ear. But when Jack had thought about opening the jar on the trip back, she had swiped at the back of his neck. It had been extremely effective — the jar remained unopened, and Jack's neck had a dozen (very nasty) blood-streaked gashes. He was definitely going to cut her claws when he got back home.

Jack put down the jar and fished in his pockets for his house key. He eventually found it, along with a handful of soil. He pushed the dirt-encrusted key into the shiny brass lock. The door swung open in a smooth arc, and Jack breathed a sigh of relief. Here it was. Warmth. TV. Home. He was safe.

At that moment his phone beeped—it was working again! He saw that he had several text messages. One was from his friend Ayo, who had received the picture Jack sent him of the empty train. He had sent a long message back teasing Jack for having to spend a holiday in the middle of nowhere with an old lady. Jack quickly typed something equally insulting, sent the text, then pocketed his phone, intending to read his other messages later.

He wandered into the hallway and saw that his mom's coat was missing from the hook next to the door. She was a nurse, so she was either out on a hospital shift or meeting one of her many friends for a cup of tea.

He dropped his suitcase on the floor before walking into the kitchen. Then he carefully placed the cookie jar on the shelf above the fridge, where it seemed to shimmer with the sweet smell of baking. Jack heard another key turn in the front door, and his dad's heavy footsteps rang through the house. Timmy, the family Labrador, bounded into the kitchen barking madly. He then sat drooling at Jack's feet, looking up at him in adoration.

The white cat jumped onto the floor from Jack's shoulder. Carefully, she pressed her nose to Timmy's. The poor dog jumped backward and landed awkwardly. The cat made a noise that sounded suspiciously like a chuckle and tiptoed over to the astonished dog. Jack left them to become friends and walked into the living room to see his dad.

"Hiya, Dad, I'm back!"

His father turned around at the sound of Jack's voice. He was sitting in an armchair in front of the fire. He did not look happy.

The smile fell from Jack's face. A nasty feeling bubbled up from the bottom of his stomach.

Until six months ago, Norman Riddle had always been a thoroughly contented man. He went to work, he came home, and then he read the paper and complained loudly about the youth of today. (Jack was included in this category). Jack used to roll his eyes, then go with his dad for Indian takeout as a special treat, during which they would argue good-naturedly about what they would watch on TV that night. Jack had loved walking to the restaurant with his dad — it was a time just for them. They would buy an extra meat samosa and split it on the way back, watching the steam from the hot pastry cool like dragon's breath in the evening air.

But then Mr. Riddle started to lose work. The restaurant where he worked as a chef had cut back his hours. When there were extra shifts available, he came home late covered in flour and cheerfully called for his dinner. When there were no shifts, he came home early. Jack hated those evenings, because his dad was always in a terrible mood.

And right now Mr. Riddle was not pleased. He stared at

his son. "What are you doing home so early? I thought you were staying with your aunt for two more days!"

Jack opened his mouth to answer, but his dad carried on talking over him. "It's bad enough that we had to practically beg the school to let you have a few days off during term time, what with your aunt saying she wasn't too well and all. But you've not even managed to stay where you were supposed to be! Your poor old aunt was really looking forward to seeing you. Said she loves young people — that she could just gobble them up! Weird way of putting it; that's what your mother said when she told me about the conversation, but I suppose your poor aunt's so old that she's going to sound a bit different. And another thing —"

Mr. Riddle drew a huge breath, and Jack braced himself for another lecture on how Jack had let everyone down. But the shouting never came. Mr. Riddle suddenly seemed confused and said, "Where'd you get that cat?"

Jack looked down and saw the white cat twined around his feet. To Jack's astonishment, Mr. Riddle broke into a smile and said, "Well, that looks pure pedigree. Bet we could get a nice price for that cat."

The cat arched her back and hissed.

Jack scooped her up and said, "No! You can't sell her!" He made his way to the sofa and sank into its cushiony depths, holding the cat on his knee. His hands trembled, so he stroked her fur to hide them. He really hated arguing with his dad. And he had no idea why he was making such a fuss about keeping the cat. All she seemed to do was cause him trouble. But for some reason, he felt much safer with her around. *Not that I need to feel safe,* he thought hurriedly.

Mr. Riddle glared at him for a moment, then reached down and picked up the TV remote control.

"Oh well," he said. "You look after the dog pretty well. I guess a cat won't be too much for you."

Jack gave a hesitant smile.

Then Mr. Riddle snapped, "Is there anything else I need to know about? A herd of elephants stashed in your backpack, perhaps?"

Jack thought of the cookie jar safely stowed away in the kitchen. He thought about telling his dad the whole story, but stopped when he saw his dad's scowl. "Uh, nothing else, nothing interesting."

Raising one eyebrow, Mr. Riddle said, "So why'd you come home so early? Bored?" He nodded sympathetically.

Encouraged, Jack decided to try confiding in his dad. "Aunt Gee Gee is just so . . . weird. She lives in a forest and owns millions of cats, just like a — uh, well, like a witch."

The minute Jack uttered the "w" word, he regretted it. If there was anything his dad loathed, it was what he called "airy-fairy stuff and nonsense."

But Mr. Riddle just threw back his head and roared with laughter. "A witch? *A witch?* That's the dumbest thing I've heard all year! Next you'll be telling me that cat can juggle!"

Mr. Riddle had tears of laughter running down his red cheeks, and Jack felt even smaller.

"Yeah," Jack laughed weakly. "Just what I thought. Really. Who believes in that stuff? Anyway, I'm going to play some video games. See you later. . . ."

While his dad was still rocking with laughter, Jack stood up and crept out the door. He slunk upstairs to his room and collapsed on his bed. The cat followed him, then daintily curled up into a ball on his pillow and began to snore. Jack stared at the ceiling and thought his dad had a point. A witch? Of course his aunt wasn't a witch! He really didn't know why he'd said that. Even if he hadn't passed out and dreamed the whole thing, there must be some kind of normal explanation. Maybe the spooky atmosphere in the forest had caused him to think the worst. Maybe she just loved animals. Maybe she was just a terrible cook. Maybe the carousel had been a play or something she and her friends were rehearsing and he, after watching too many scary movies, had thought it was some kind of evil coven.

Despite this list of perfectly acceptable ideas, doubts began to filter back into his head. He still couldn't explain the goblin. Was he really just an eccentric local? There was an old man on his street who wore garbage bags on his feet and talked loudly to the pigeons. Maybe the man in the tree was like him. Jack shook his head and decided not to worry about it anymore. He was home. He didn't have to go back there ever again. Plus he had a new pet.

And he could go to school tomorrow. This wasn't something that would normally interest him. But the thought of doing something so, well, normal, made Jack hug his pillow in relief.

Jack grabbed his phone and spent a good half hour texting and checking his social media accounts. His fingers rapidly tapped away at the screen as he felt himself sink back into his life. He arranged to go and play soccer with a few of his friends that weekend. They weren't very good. In fact they usually just spent an hour half-heartedly kicking a ball around the deserted fields behind the school. The real treat was the trip to McDonald's afterward, which is where most of the local kids went on the weekends. They would gobble their favorite burgers with extra ketchup, then spend the rest of the afternoon hanging around outside with anyone else who showed up.

This done, he leaped up from the bed and went into the bathroom to brush his teeth. His mind went back to his aunt as he scrubbed. *She really is the worst cook I've ever met.* He was used to his dad's cooking, which was always wonderful no matter what ingredients he tossed in. Jack spat blue foam into the sink and licked away the flecks of toothpaste still stuck to his lips. *Those cookies do smell amazing though,* he thought longingly.

He padded out of the bathroom and jumped into bed. *I know she told me not to eat them, but she must've been joking. Maybe she meant that she just didn't want me to eat them on the way home.*

She wanted me to wait until I got back so I could share them. Jack pulled the blanket up over his shoulders and decided that he would take the cookies to school tomorrow and share them with his friends. With this cheerful, (and, he thought, very generous) idea, Jack slid into a deep sleep.

Downstairs, in the cold, silent kitchen, the cookie jar trembled on the shelf.

Its lid was moving.

* * *

The next day dawned bright and sunny. To Jack, the world seemed to be perfect. He walked along the road to school, whistling through his teeth. In his school bag, he carried the cookie jar and the scent of newly baked cookies wafted to his nose.

The only bad part of the day so far had been the cat's reaction when he was about to leave the house. She had tried to jump on his shoulder. After he had told her she absolutely could not come to school, the cat sat on her haunches and howled like a wolf. Jack had ignored her and shut the door firmly.

Jack felt a little uncomfortable as he thought about the cat. He hadn't realized that cats could howl. Or understand speech. *If the cat isn't normal, then maybe I really did see something strange in the forest,* he thought anxiously. But he quickly forgot these dark thoughts as his school came into view. It was impossible to think of anything imaginative at his school. The teachers discouraged that kind of thing.

Jack went to the local secondary school, a solid red-brick building. The principal, Mr. Scrimp, rarely smiled. There was a rumor that he was a failed professional tennis player. He'd been scouted as a boy and favored to be the next Wimbledon champion, but a knee injury had ended his career early. After giving up tennis in the 1980s, he had piled on the pounds and had been on a diet ever since.

These days he delighted in souring everyone's day so they felt as miserable as he did. He always held early meetings on a Monday and late meetings on a Friday, which the staff were never quite brave enough to complain about. The pupils avoided him when they could, because he was fanatical about getting them to realize their sporting potential. He forced them to try every after-school sport (even if they were clearly useless at that sport). Jack had lost count of the number of evenings he had spent, soaked to the skin, running around and around the soccer field in an effort to keep up with the others in cross-country. And he had pretty much blocked out the horror that was basketball. With his (lack of) height, he had almost been trampled to death on a few occasions.

But even the thought of his grumpy principal couldn't depress Jack today. If he saw Mr. Scrimp's greasy face, he would only smile.

Jack strode through the gates and spotted his friend Liam dawdling in a corner of the playground. Liam always looked like someone had struck him across the head — dazed, confused, and half asleep. This was the result of far too many late-night gaming sessions carried out under the cover of darkness, so his parents wouldn't realize what he was up to.

Liam saw Jack and grinned. He ambled over and said, "Where've you been? It's been boring here, as usual."

Jack had told Liam where he was going, but Liam had obviously forgotten. Students milled around them, shuffling through the school doors as the clock struck nine.

"Jack!" a voice called.

He turned around to see one of his other friends, Ayo, wrinkling his nose to stop his glasses falling down. Ayo loathed his glasses and swore he was going to get contacts once he was old enough — and had gotten over his fear of accidentally gouging out his own eyeballs.

Ayo came over to Jack with a girl named Hannah, who had long blond hair in a tight ponytail. Casually, she swung her schoolbag in a circle, cracking two other students across the shoulder. She ignored their cries and carried on walking.

Jack watched her swinging bag carefully. No matter how many times people complained, she still managed to smack somebody with it at least twice a day. He'd given up mentioning it and just tried to duck at the right moment.

"What was the trip like? Terrible as you thought it'd be?" Ayo grinned.

Jack rolled his eyes. "Terrible," he agreed. He had decided not to tell his friends about the more . . . unusual stuff. He was determined to forget about it.

"As bad as math?" Liam asked.

"Worse," Jack replied.

They chatted for a few more minutes, then Ayo and Hannah walked ahead of them. Both were always in detention for being late to school and had been threatened with the dreaded community service detention if they were late again. This meant cleaning up litter or scrubbing pots in the cafeteria — on a Friday after school.

Liam and Jack ambled toward their classroom, hoping to shave a few minutes off the hour of Monday morning torture. Jack told Liam about his latest video game. Liam's eyes grew wide, and he interrupted with "Wow" and "No way!" every five seconds. They headed down the hallway, so engrossed that they didn't notice the principal until they walked into him.

"Ooooommmph!"

The boys bounced off Mr. Scrimp's stomach and fell to the floor. Jack's bag slid off his shoulder and burst open, scattering pens, old sandwich wrappers, and the cookie jar onto the floor.

"Sorry, sir," the boys mumbled, scrambling to their feet.

Mr. Scrimp straightened his shoulders, pretending he wasn't horribly winded. "Make sure you look where you're going in the hallways! You could seriously hurt someone if you just mosey along with your heads in the clouds." He gestured to Jack's belongings, strewn across the floor. "And look at this mess! Health and safety nightmare, you know. Well, come on, pick it up!"

"Uh, yeah, sure," Jack said, ducking down. He shoved his things back into the bag and reached for the cookie jar.

"What on earth is that?" Mr. Scrimp asked with a frown.

"Uh, cookies, sir," Jack said. "My aunt baked them."

Mr. Scrimp sniffed through his hairy nostrils. "You know full well that cookies aren't allowed in this school. We have a healthy eating policy — that means no refined sugar." He held out his hand. "I'll have to confiscate those, I'm afraid. You'll thank me for it when you're older and have no cavities. Come on, quick, quick. The first class is about to start."

Jack reluctantly handed over the cookie jar.

The principal nodded and marched off to his office, leaving Jack staring after him, mourning his treat. Liam simply shuffled off down the hall, yawning.

His shoulders hunched, Jack trudged to his class, ignoring the shrieks coming from the classrooms around him. Logic told him he had nothing to worry about — it was just a jar of cookies — but he couldn't help feeling as if something very bad was about to happen.

CHAPTER 7

MR. SCRIMP'S NASTY ORDEAL

Around the hall corner, another man had watched the scene in astonishment. He saw Mr. Scrimp pick up the cookie jar and gasped in shock. He crept back to his own office, a tiny and dusty room filled with ancient books. Normally teachers had to use the faculty lounge, but he had been given his own office. None of the other teachers liked talking to him, because they thought he was a bit strange. His office was an ex-custodian's closet, tucked away at a far end of the school. This usually suited him just fine; he didn't like the other teachers either. But he'd come out to see what all the fuss was about — and he wished he'd never left his cozy office.

Horrified, the man sat at his desk and stared at the human skull he was using as a paperweight. Hundreds of leather-bound books lined the walls, which he normally spent many happy hours reading. But his thoughts were far away, thinking of the jar.

"It can't be!" he whispered. "It just can't be . . . not after all this time, all these centuries . . . could it be the witch's jar?"

He ran to his overflowing bookshelf and grabbed an ancient-looking notebook. Quickly he flicked through the pages, muttering feverishly to himself. Finally he found the page he was looking for. There was an old drawing of a ceramic jar, with lines of dense, spidery handwriting underneath it. He gasped. "It is! It really is the witch's jar! We're all in danger! It can't be opened, not again, or some poor soul will be doomed!"

He jumped to his feet and turned toward the door. Unfortunately he tripped over the tiger-skin rug on the floor and fell, cracking his head on the desk. As he lost consciousness, he began to dream of jester's bells, witches, and chocolate.

* * *

Mr. Scrimp was not happy. He marched back to his tidy office and gently placed the cookie jar on his gleaming desk. Then he sighed and sat down in his comfortable chair. The leather creaked as he leaned back. He laced his fingers behind his head and stared out the window. This was the time of the day he liked most, when he didn't have to deal with behavior issues, angry parents, or unhappy teachers. There was a sticky note taped to his laptop reminding him to call back the teachers' union representative, but he decided to put it off for a while. The silence of his office was incredibly soothing.

Mr. Scrimp quickly checked his calendar to make sure he

didn't have any meetings in the next hour, then leaned down to grab a pair of headphones from underneath his desk.

He didn't notice the lid on the cookie jar sliding gently back and forth.

Just before he sat up, the lid stopped moving.

Mr. Scrimp plugged his headphones into his cell phone (which he had banned both students and teachers from using in school. The administrators had all agreed that phones were a terrible distraction. But he decided that, as the principal, he could excuse himself from this rule) and turned on his favorite music. He closed his eyes and lost himself in a familiar daydream. It was summer, and he was playing at Wimbledon. The crowd was cheering his name. He sprinted across the court, his knee miraculously healed.

The crowd roared in approval as he effortlessly won each game.

Thwock, thwock, went the ball.

He waved at his adoring fans. They went crazy, standing to scream "SCRIMP! WE LOVE YOU, SCRIMP!"

The sun beat down and he shielded his eyes to better see the people in the crowd.

Then the smell of freshly baking cookies wafted across the courts . . .

Mr. Scrimp blinked and pulled off his headphones. *Hang on*, he thought. *Baking? At Wimbledon?*

Slowly he sat up and stared at the jar on his desk. There

was no doubt about it; he could smell sweet dough and fresh, gooey, chocolate chips.

Mr. Scrimp was on a diet because he loved sugar too much. His metal lunch box by the door contained a single Mars bar — he usually only allowed himself one candy bar a week. But one measly candy bar really wasn't enough. *And homemade treats beat a supermarket candy bar hands down,* he thought longingly. Mr. Scrimp inhaled deeply and thought Jack's aunt must be the most wonderful cook in the universe. *Perhaps I should just try one,* he thought, *to see what it tastes like. It would be a shame to waste such delicious baking. And really, I'm saving my pupils' teeth by eating the cookies myself.*

He eagerly leaned toward the jar and put one hand on the lid. Gripping the lid, he pulled on the heavy piece of pottery. The heavenly smell became stronger, and he thrust his other hand in the jar to grab a cookie.

And just as fast, he whipped it out again, his heart hammering in his chest. There was something moving around in the jar!

He heard a small, strange voice that sounded like trees creaking in a forest at midnight.

"Smaaaaasssssshhhhh awaaaaakkkkke . . ."

Mr. Scrimp fell backward off his seat. He hit the floor with a thump and gawked, unable to believe his eyes.

A gnarled hand came out of the jar and rested on the edge. Two tarnished brass bells rose above the hand, followed by a hat that was split in two.

It's a jester's hat, thought poor Mr. Scrimp.

The creature that wore the hat had a leathery face with skin like a piece of parchment — old, wrinkled, and the color of a tea stain. Tiny black eyes like blackberries squinted at the principal, and its mouth opened to reveal jagged, sharp teeth.

It wheezed, "Smaaaaasssssshhhhh ooooouuuuuttttt!" and giggled helplessly as it pulled the rest of its body out of the jar. Landing on the desk, it crouched. It wore brown leather shoes with upturned toes and was about a foot tall. Mr. Scrimp stared at its clothes: it wore a suit with faded red and black stripes, topped with a white ruffle around its throat.

"What are you?" croaked Mr. Scrimp.

The creature cackled, "ME SMASH! SMASH! SMASH, SMASH, SMASH!" It leaped off the desk onto the floor and began to hop from one foot to another, chanting, "SMASH, smash, SMASH, smash, SMASH!" The bells on its hat jangled in time to the chant. Mr. Scrimp had never heard such a horrible sound.

Blackberry eyes twinkling, it danced over to Mr. Scrimp's metal lunch box by the door. It ripped off the lid and threw the contents on the floor, wrinkling its nose at the lettuce sandwich and apple. But when it came across the Mars bar, it whooped in delight and began to tear off the wrapper.

Mr. Scrimp snapped out of his horrified trance and shouted, "Hey! That's mine!"

The principal was outraged. He had lived on lettuce and fruit for a week, and his one treat was about to be stolen! He had planned to eat it a little at a time, drowning in the delicious naughtiness of the forbidden sugar.

Heaving himself to his feet, he lunged across the room and snatched the candy bar from the creature's leathery paw. It glared at him and gnashed its teeth in fury. Mr. Scrimp realized the danger and made a sensible decision.

He ran.

He raced from the office clutching the precious candy bar to his chest. The creature roared in anger and chased Mr. Scrimp, howling, "SMASHSMASHSMASHSMASHSMASH!"

They made an interesting sight as they thundered through the school hallways — Mr. Scrimp screeching like a toddler, closely followed by a furious, tiny creature dressed like a jester.

* * *

Meanwhile Jack was on the other side of the school in his math class, trying to learn algebra, (and, if he was being honest, trying not to worry about the cookie jar). His droning teacher Mr. Batra was presenting a PowerPoint presentation that had endless bullet points.

Jack gazed round the room.

Ayo had his head on his desk and was busily scratching his initials in the plastic. Hannah was hunched forward in her seat staring fixedly at the board, as if by looking at it long enough, the words would somehow make sense. She caught Jack's eye and slowly put her head down, miming banging her head on the desk. Jack stifled a laugh, then turned around in his seat to see what other people were doing.

Some of the students were still trying hopelessly to understand the lesson, while the rest had given up and nodded off. Liam was sound asleep with his mouth open, in danger of drooling on his desk. Many students had their phones out and were tapping away at them, ready to tuck them away at a second's notice when the teacher turned around. Jack decided that was the best idea and reached into his pocket to pull out his own phone.

Then there was a commotion in the hall, which grew louder with every passing second. There was the sound of thumping, jangling bells and a pitter-patter of tiny feet.

They all gaped at each other. Liam, who had been openly snoring, jerked awake crying, "Waaazzat?"

The noise in the hall grew louder. There was a strange jingling, as if an elephant was playing the tambourine.

Some of the braver students got up from their desks and tiptoed past Mr. Batra. He was facing the whiteboard and far too interested in talking about algebra to notice a little thing like half his class leaving the room.

Jack joined them and peered round the door. His blood ran cold as the uncomfortable sense of foreboding he had experienced earlier grew stronger.

The strange noise was getting louder and louder and louder.

Ayo walked up next to him. "What d'you think that is?" he asked, pushing his glasses up his nose.

All of a sudden Mr. Scrimp raced past, clutching a Mars bar

and shrieking, "It came from the jar I tell you! CALL THE ZOO! Call the zoooo!"

Then Jack saw a flash of red and black stripes zoom past — it was a tiny figure, furiously chasing the principal and whooping. The children all began to talk at once, thrilled at the drama.

Mr. Batra jumped and turned around from the board. Seeing that his students were actually trying to escape, he boomed, "What are you all doing? Get. Back. In. Here. At. ONCE!"

The kids ignored him. Ayo grabbed Jack's arm. "Did you see that? That was crazy! Who d'you think was chasing him? Has a really angry parent finally lost it, d'you think?"

"Uh . . . ," Jack faltered.

Hannah scrambled up next to them. "He looked so scared! Do you think he's doing some new sprint training program or something? You know, like, they get some kind of robot to chase us and make us go faster?"

"Um, maybe," Jack replied.

Liam hopped from one leg to another, too agitated to stand still. "You're all wrong!" he said. "That wasn't no animal, or, I dunno, some sort of robot dreamed up by a really evil PE teacher. That was a-a-a thing! It wasn't normal — or natural!"

Ayo rolled his eyes, but Jack felt as if all the air had suddenly left his lungs. *Not normal,* he thought. All the little things started to add up like one giant, awful jigsaw puzzle.

The creepy house. The cats. The black hat. The cauldron carousel. The eerie mist.

Jack stared silently at the other children as they chattered. Mr. Batra was trying, unsuccessfully, to get some sense out of his class, but they were all stumbling over each other in their eagerness to tell him what they had seen.

"It was a dog, sir! It was one of those pit bull thingies!" cried one girl with long braids.

"No, don't listen to her! It was that high school boy who got expelled — he's back for revenge!" said the student standing next to her, a serious expression on his face.

Jack gulped and stayed silent, although he thought he knew the truth. The whole school had heard Mr. Scrimp say the creature chasing him had come from the jar. Whatever it was, that thing had come from his aunt.

And it was meant for him.

* * *

While Mr. Batra battled to control his class and refused to believe any of the wild stories he was being told, poor Mr. Scrimp was running furiously all round the school. He was trying desperately to shake off the determined creature behind him. He didn't know — or care — what it was; he just wanted it to leave him alone. His authority was fading with every undignified step he took, his face burning with humiliation. Also, Mr. Scrimp hadn't exercised since 1982.

The gabbling creature was quickly gaining on him and Mr. Scrimp decided to take drastic action. He used his last ounce of energy to speed up and burst through the swinging metal doors marked PLAYGROUND. It was empty, but children peered through the windows all over the school building, eager to see what Mr. Scrimp would do next.

Led by the teachers, they had all left their classes to watch. They couldn't miss this. Even Mr. Batra gave up trying to explain his beloved algebra. He joined the students, who had their faces pressed to the windows. He gasped with amazement.

"OK guys, get away from the windows." Pause. "We're going next door for a better look."

The class cheered and crowded into a double classroom that had massive windows overlooking the playground.

Jack and Ayo elbowed their way to the front and wrestled open one of the windows so they could hear what was going on. Hannah and Liam pushed their way forward and peered over their shoulders.

Jack watched anxiously as the principal and the creature sped out into the playground. Mr. Scrimp screeched to a halt in the center of the playground, wisps of smoke drifting from the heels of his smart black shoes. The creature almost collided with Mr. Scrimp's back, but swerved neatly at the last minute. It crouched down in front of him and grinned, its black eyes flashing and fingers curling into claws.

Mr. Scrimp stared the thing straight in the eye, cleared his throat, unwrapped the candy bar . . . and stuffed it into his mouth. He began to chew the bar whole. Watery chocolate trailed from his mouth onto his collar. The creature howled with rage, and the children pressed their noses eagerly against the glass.

Jack groaned. He knew that whatever was going to happen next wouldn't be good. Mr. Scrimp chewed methodically like a cow as the creature screeched its disappointment. His mouth, chin, and shirt were covered in brown juice. It dripped down his front and splashed on the ground.

The creature suddenly fell silent and contemplated the ground, its bells jangling softly. Mr. Scrimp grinned through bulging cheeks. *Aha!* he thought triumphantly. *No one gets the better of Rupert Scrimp! Nobod—*

Mr. Scrimp was cut off mid-thought as the creature raised its head with a jerk. It bared its teeth and muttered, "Smash . . . smash . . . smashsmashSMAAASH!"

It leaped through the air, its hands together like a diver. Mr. Scrimp's eyes almost popped out of his head as the grinning creature came flying toward him . . . and disappeared headfirst down his throat, leaving only two tiny feet sticking out of the principal's mouth. With a popping sound, they then disappeared completely.

The children gasped, and the teachers screamed.

"Eeeeewwwww!" Hannah shouted. "That's so gross!"

Mr. Scrimp stood paralyzed, his mouth open and his eyes bulging. Jack snapped out of his trance and leaped away from the window.

"Where're you going? We've got the best view here!" Hannah asked.

Jack ignored her and pushed his way through the crowd, ran into the hall, and then jumped down the stairs, two at a time. He had no idea what he was going to do, but he knew he had to help.

He pushed open the doors to the playground. Mr. Scrimp stood where Jack had last seen him, his eyes wide and unseeing. Cautiously Jack walked up to the principal and took a deep breath. Mr. Scrimp looked like he was made of stone, with his white, shocked face.

Jack quietly circled the principal. Catcalls and shouts came from the windows and a few boos. Jack was fairly certain the teachers were the ones booing.

Jack warily studied the silent principal. The shouts from the windows died down, and the whole school stood quietly, just waiting to see what would happen next. A cold wind blew dead leaves across the playground. Jack was considering whether to try slapping him when an eerie giggling came from Mr. Scrimp. But his mouth wasn't moving.

The giggle came from his stomach.

Jack felt the hair on the back of his neck rise at the sound. Then it stopped, and the playground was silent.

"BLEEEERUUGH!" A huge stream of yellow, smelly vomit flew out of Mr. Scrimp's mouth.

Jack jumped out of the way. "Urgh! Yuck!"

The vomit ran down Mr. Scrimp's tie and shirt and sloshed

over his feet. His mouth widened in a horrified O.

Jack took a step back and held his nose, trying not to gag at the vile smell.

"BBBBBLLLLLEEEEERRRRR!"

Another, more revolting stream of vomit came out. Except this time, the creature came with it. It was surfing on several chunks of undigested Mars bar. Its hands were above its head, and it whooped as it hit the ground.

Mr. Scrimp stood goggle-eyed for a moment . . . then his eyes rolled back into his head and he fell over, crashing headfirst into the vomit.

The creature dodged the falling figure of the poor principal. It cackled in glee, dripping yellow goo as it danced around Mr. Scrimp's body.

"SMAAAAASH!" it howled. Then it crouched on all fours and sniffed the air. Its eyes widened, and it grinned, flashing jagged teeth. "Ummmmm, Ssssssmmashhhhh smeeeeellllls suuuuuggggggaaaaarrrrr," it whispered.

Jack watched as the creature swayed away from him and toddled across the playground. The last thing Jack saw was the tarnished bells on its hat twinkling in the sun as it leaped over the school wall.

At that moment an ambulance siren wailed in the distance.

CHAPTER 8

PROFESSOR AMBROSIUS FOOTNOTE

While Mr. Scrimp was taken to hospital, Jack was furiously trying to come up with a plan. He had to do something to catch the creature! He had brought it here; he was to blame. And his parents would kill him if they ever found out he'd had something to do with it. But what could he do? Already the teachers and other children had decided the creature must be some kind of wild monkey. One of the PE teachers had contacted the zoo, and the school echoed with her shouts of, "What do you mean 'not possible'? Are you calling me a liar, sir?"

Liam was even ignoring Jack's protests, saying the creature was definitely an alien. But Jack knew better. He was sure it was some kind of goblin, like the one in the tree, but this one was insane. He just didn't know what to do or who to tell. No one would believe him if he told them. Ayo and Hannah would just look at him oddly, then shrug and walk off to their next class.

Jack walked glumly back up to his classroom, taking the stairs two at a time and listening to Liam jabbering about spaceships, when he noticed something odd. Professor Footnote's door was open.

The professor had a reputation for being strange. He rambled about fairy tales all day. He taught history and was the only teacher who was a professor — the others were all Mr. or Ms. He never joined the other teachers in the faculty lounge, instead shutting himself in his office. He had given strict orders that no one was to disturb him there — and when he was out, it was locked.

Jack slowed his steps. Liam carried on, still talking. Jack waited until Liam had wandered down the hall, then peered around the door of the professor's office. With a gasp he ran inside.

"Professor! Are you all right? Did it get you too?"

Professor Footnote was on the floor, lying on a tiger-skin rug, his head next to the desk. He was unconscious, but thankfully there was no vomit. *Not the goblin then,* Jack thought grimly.

The professor raised his head, said "Umph," and seemed to realize where he was. He shot to his feet with a cry — and promptly banged his head on a hanging glass globe.

Jack winced in sympathy. "Are you OK? Do you want a

drink of water or, I dunno, an aspirin or something?"

Not for the first time, Jack thought how odd the professor was. He had tufts of thick white hair, which constantly stood on end like a halo. His brown eyes rolled like a panicky horse behind a pair of wire-rimed glasses on his elastic face, which always pulled the funniest expressions.

The professor turned and focused on Jack for the first time. He grabbed Jack by the collar and dragged him closer. "You! I know you! You're the boy with the jar! The jar!"

Jack pulled away from the professor's grip and backed up. "What d'you mean?" he squeaked. "What d'you know about it?"

"I know everything, you silly boy! But *you* don't know what could happen!" the professor gasped, grabbing Jack's collar again. "You must give it to me, and quickly, before it's opened — or we will all be in danger!"

Jack's heart sank to his feet.

The professor saw Jack's face and realized the truth. He let go and backed away, putting his hand over his mouth. "Oh no. No, no, no . . ." he whispered.

Jack was miserable and defensive. "None of this is my fault! I didn't ask for this weird stuff to happen!"

Professor Footnote's hand fell from his mouth and he looked a bit shamefaced. "Of course, of course. You're just a boy. I sometimes forget what it is to be young." He nodded at Jack to sit down. Jack sat on a chair and stared at the floor.

The professor said, "You're not the first, and you won't be

the last, to fall for the witch's tricks. Unless . . ."

Jack frowned. How did he know about Aunt Gee Gee? He hadn't said anything.

The professor carried on. "There could be a way . . . Although others have tried before . . . Perhaps with my help . . . Maybe the lad could . . ." His voice trailed off. He looked sharply at Jack and raised one bushy white eyebrow. "Worth a try, I suppose," he mused. Then he reached across and snapped on a lamp. He swung it around so Jack was blinded by the glare.

The professor sat opposite Jack and barked, "Where did you get the jar?"

Blinking, Jack scowled, irritated by the professor's sudden mood swings. "Why should I tell you?"

"Because if you don't, you'll go down in history as a warning to badly behaved children."

"What's *that* supposed to mean?"

"Answer my question!"

"*No!* You're as weird as she is!"

The professor did look strange: his white hair stood on end even more than usual, and his eyes flashed. Perhaps he realized this. His hand relaxed, and he moved the light so it was no longer blinding Jack. The professor mumbled another apology.

Sighing heavily, he sank back into his chair. He picked up a teacup from the table next to him with trembling hands and drained the cup. "I know you are very confused by all this, but you have to believe that I'm the only one who can help you. Here — you must be thirsty. The shock, you realize. Drink this."

The professor reached into his bag and pulled out a bottle of water, which he slid over the desk to Jack.

Jack chewed his bottom lip. Should he trust the professor? He wasn't sure. To buy time (and because he really was quite thirsty; he didn't normally spend his days running around the school), he reached over for the bottle of water and cracked open the lid. Taking a sip of the lukewarm drink, he made up his mind.

"Professor," he began.

"Oh please, call me Ambrosius. Professor sounds so serious."

Jack paused. "Your name is Professor Ambrosius Footnote?"

"Yes. And?"

Jack's mouth twitched. "Um, nothing. Just think I'll stick with professor. . . ."

The professor stood up and began to pace up and down his office, muttering under his breath. Jack's eyes wandered to the bookcases. The books were moldy and had titles like *Fairy Tale or Fiction?* and *Discovering the Eerie Truth Behind the Monstrous Myths*.

Then Jack's phone beeped, making him jump. He fumbled to open it and saw a message from Hannah. It was a picture of Liam asleep, his head on his desk, with his mouth wide open.

Ayo was carefully drawing a mustache above the sleeping boy's lip, joining up the blue and red beard that had already been scrawled all over his chin. Clearly the teachers had given up trying to discipline the students for the day. There was a message underneath that said:

Where are you?? Get here before he wakes up, lol!

He looked up. The professor raised an eyebrow at him.

"Sorry," Jack said hastily. He hoped the professor wouldn't confiscate his phone. He was normally really good at hiding his phone at school.

The professor stopped pacing and watched Jack with a speculative expression.

He strode over to the chair opposite and placed his trembling hands on the table. "Fine. I'll tell you the whole story. Without my help you will certainly be doomed — and you probably are anyway. But you have to promise me you'll tell me where you got the jar. And who gave it to you," he added darkly.

Jack nodded. He needed to find out what was going on. But he had a horrible feeling he wouldn't like the story, especially now that he'd been told he was doomed for some reason. He hoped it was just the professor being dramatic. . . .

The professor closed his eyes and drew a deep breath. "Do you believe in fairy tales?"

Jack was uncertain. "What, like Disney movies, that kind of thing? Or the ones you talk about in class?"

The professor shook his head impatiently. "Not the

namby-pamby, happily-ever-after ones those ridiculous movies tell you about. I mean the ones with teeth and claws. The real ones." He paused. "This one starts with a hanging."

Outside, rain had begun to fall. It pattered against the glass, sounding like someone was tapping on the window. The professor picked up a plaid thermos from his desk, unscrewed the lid and poured the steaming contents into his chipped teacup. He took a thoughtful sip.

"It began long ago. I suppose you could say 'once upon a time.' It really began in a little village in Sheffield in 1610 when a woman was hanged for witchcraft. But many men and women died horrible deaths at that time, so what made this one any different?

"In 1610 King James ruled England. He was a frightened man who feared magic above anything else. Both of his parents were murdered, and he was convinced the powers of darkness had killed them — and wanted him dead too.

"He published a book about monsters, and people were so terrified of him — he was as mad as a box of frogs, by the way, and tended to chop people's heads off when they disagreed with him — they said the book was amazing. Big mistake."

The professor paused to take another sip of his tea, then continued. "This encouraged the king to try to get rid of all the evil in the land. He started by bringing in witch hunters. They were vile men who went to villages and accused people, usually women, of being witches. If you were accused, you had no hope of proving your innocence. They would throw you in a river to see if you drowned, because witches were supposed to be able to call for help from the evil spirits that lived in the water. These spirits were thought to make a witch float. If you didn't drown, you would be called a witch and you would killed by your own neighbors anyway. They were dark times."

Jack shivered. The professor spoke as if he had been there. The fear in his voice made Jack's own unease deepen.

"People used the witch hunt as an excuse to accuse someone they didn't like — or wanted to get rid of. And this brings us to the village in Sheffield. A woman lived alone in the woods and healed the villagers with ancient magic. She liked to live away from other people so she could talk to the birds and the trees. She would visit the villagers and bring them medicine when they were sick, which she made from secret herbs growing in her garden. At first she was praised by the people for her wonderful cures, but then something awful happened."

The professor ran his fingers through his hair. Jack noticed they were still trembling.

"This woman also made wonderful sweets. She knew everything about cooking, and she baked cakes, cookies, and chocolates. She gave them away to the village children, who had never even tasted sugar before. The woman left them outside her house on stone trays, and children would come from miles around to grab the sweets — sticky toffees, crumbly cakes, and gooey chocolates. One day two children, a brother and a sister, visited her. But the brother and sister were not normal children. Their names were Hansel and Gretel."

Jack started, sitting up in his seat. "What? Hang on! They're the good guys! Everyone knows that!"

The professor scowled. "Do you mind? I was just getting warmed up! But yes, they are remembered as brave children. People say they were abandoned by their parents and captured by a witch who wanted to eat them, but Gretel pushed the witch into an oven and both children were saved. Am I right?"

"Well, yes, of course!" Jack was not impressed. He'd heard that story many times. He folded his arms and started to wonder if the professor was all right in the head. He thought about what excuse he could make to leave. Clearly the professor wasn't going to be able to help him.

The professor snorted and threw his hands in the air. "PROPAGANDA! STUFF AND NONSENSE! LIES, ALL LIES!" he shouted.

Jack flinched. *He seriously has more mood swings than Aunt Gee Gee,* he thought.

The professor gave a bitter laugh and said, "It was all a cover-up to hide the truth — the terrible truth." He paused. "Shall I continue?"

Reluctantly, Jack nodded. He was here now, so he might as well hear the rest. And the professor was between him and the door. . . .

"Right, where was I? Oh yes, Hansel and Gretel. They were both greedy children, but in different ways. Hansel wanted the sweets. He couldn't stop eating all that sugar. I have it on good authority that he was a very overweight child — a professor in London telephones me sometimes when he just *has* to talk about his research; he's rather annoying, actually — but Gretel was thin and pale. All she wanted was the woman's power.

"Gretel was a nasty child — the sort who sets other little girls' hair on fire because they're prettier than she is. She wanted to make herself powerful and make people scared of her. But she didn't understand how the woman had got her magic. So she asked her where she found her power. The woman smiled and said nothing. She knew Gretel would grow up to be a vile person. There was no way she would give away such an important secret to a horrible little girl."

The professor was becoming more animated, color flooding into his cheeks as he told the story. He jumped to his feet and started to act it out.

"Gretel was so angry that the woman refused to share the secret of her power, she made her brother go with her to the witch hunters. She stood before a court and told them she had escaped from the woman's house. She said the woman had fattened up her brother and intended to eat him. The court gasped — they all agreed the boy was very large. How could a boy get so big? It must be because that strange woman wanted to eat him!

"The very next day, men with torches and swords went to the woman's cottage. They took her from the house and hanged her on the village green. According to one of my sources, Gretel actually sat underneath the gallows and watched the poor woman be hanged.

"Afterward, in the dead of night, Gretel crept back to the woman's cottage and searched it, finding and taking the source of the woman's power. It was a magical wand made from a black unicorn's horn — the last of its kind before they became extinct."

Jack's eyes widened as he remembered the stick his aunt had pointed at the sky in the forest. It had looked like a curved horn made from black ivory. That had to be the stolen wand!

The professor stood still and almost whispered, "The fairy folk had given this sacred wand to the woman at a ceremony at a stone circle deep within the forest. They taught her about magic and whispered the secrets of the world into her ears, before placing the wand in the good woman's hand. And as soon as Gretel touched it, she knew about the fairies and where the wand had come from. She knew who she had stolen this power from. Then she was afraid for the first time in her nasty life.

"You see, these days, we think fairies are beautiful and sweet. But if you look at the records of them before a hundred years ago, they were actually terrifying. They were more like small monsters."

The professor swung around to the bookcase. He pulled

out a battered volume and thumbed through it, muttering under his breath. With a triumphant exclamation, he set the book down in front of Jack, who leaned forward to get a better look. There was a strange drawing on the page, sketched in black charcoal. It was a tiny woman with a cruel face and pointed ears. She was bright green and snarling, showing razor-sharp teeth and clutching a silver bow and arrow. Crouched on a tree branch and drenched in raindrops, she seemed savage . . . and frightening.

The professor watched Jack's face and nodded. He picked up the book and traced the drawing gently with his fingers while he spoke.

"The fairy folk ran wild on the hills and in the forests, wearing dead leaves as clothes and using spiderwebs to string their bows. People were frightened of them. Fairies stole children and left magical ones in their place. For their own entertainment, they scared the cows so much their milk curdled and the people starved. Gretel knew that if the fairies ever realized she had destroyed the one human they liked — well, maybe 'like' is too strong a word; respected, perhaps — they would get their revenge. But they never did come for Gretel. She started to cast evil spells with the powerful wand, which had more magic in it than you could ever imagine.

"The villagers soon learned they had made a mistake by hanging the gentle woman from the forest, because Gretel used her power to become a *real* witch. She lived in a time when people believed witches were evil and that wicked spirits walked the open roads. Gretel decided she wanted to be more evil than any witch had ever been before.

"And every story you hear about a cruel stepmother, an evil queen, or a wicked witch — it's Gretel."

Jack shifted on his chair and felt confused. What — every story? That couldn't be right. He knew plenty of people who had wicked stepparents. Also, Gretel would have to be hundreds of years old!

The professor smiled grimly at Jack. "I mean, every *fairy tale*! Her evil deeds have become legendary. She targets young children: Cinderella, Aladdin, Rapunzel, Snow White, Jack with the beanstalk. Gretel chose them all. Of course, she isn't always successful. These children all somehow managed to escape from Gretel, which is why we know about them. Snow White and Cinderella evaded her spells and married their princes. Jack slew the giant sent by Gretel to kill him. But this was rare. There are hundreds of stories with sad endings that we don't hear about. We only tell our children the success stories — not the ones where the heroes died. Or worse . . ."

Jack was getting annoyed. This had nothing to do with his problems. He had a mad goblin on the run and a strange aunt. The professor looked at him and laughed.

"Surely, lad, you see where I'm going with this?"

"Not really. And what's the deal with the cookie jar?"

"Oh," the professor replied, "didn't I mention that? The goblin from the cookie jar is Gretel's brother, Hansel. But these days he calls himself Smash — for some strange reason. I'm not sure why."

Jack was shocked. "That bonkers goblin is her brother?!"

"Gretel couldn't stand her brother, and the first thing she did was punish him for his greed. She turned him into the goblin you saw today and imprisoned him in a jar. She dressed him in a jester's outfit so everyone would laugh at him. He remembers nothing about who he is or what happened to him. All he understands is that he's hungry for sugar. And the jar is bewitched. Anyone who goes near it thinks it holds their favorite sweets."

The professor leaned forward. "So tell me lad — who gave you the jar? Was it her?"

"Uh, I think so. Well, it must've been. It was my aunt, you see."

The professor's mouth hung open. "Your aunt?!"

"Yeah. She's pretty old. Or, she's meant to be. Bit of a family myth, no one still alive had ever met her. We all thought she was this lonely old woman who wanted to meet her long lost nephew before she died." He shrugged. "Anyway, I went to visit her and she gave me the jar and told me not to open it."

"Ah, she was playing with you. She knew that by telling you not to open it, you would find it almost impossible not to. Never forget that this is all a game to her. She loves to watch children suffer."

"So is that why she wanted me to open it? Did she just

want that mad goblin to chase me like it did Mr. Scrimp, or something?"

The professor winced. "I'm afraid it's much, much worse than that, m'boy."

Jack suddenly knew the story had been leading up to this moment.

A muffled voice growled behind them. "Smash sorrrrreeeee."

Jack spun around, spilling his drink. He felt the blood drain from his face as he saw who had spoken. There, with his face squashed up against the window, was the goblin Smash.

CHAPTER 9

HANSEL AND GRETEL

Smash was squatting on the window ledge outside and grinning, showing tiny shark-like teeth. He waved madly, making the bells on the end of his hat jingle.

"Gaaaa!" Jack cried. "P-P-Professor! Call the police or something! Tell them to bring a massive net!" He leaped out of his seat and backed as far away from the window as he could get. Hastily he looked around for something heavy to chuck at the creature to knock him off the window ledge.

The professor raised an eyebrow and said, "Dear boy, what *are* you doing?"

"Doing?" Jack was halfway through weighing a dictionary. He decided it wasn't nearly heavy enough and lunged for a more solid-looking book called *The History of the British Isles: A Land of Magick*. "What do you think I'm doing? Look at what it did to Mr. Scrimp!" With shaking hands, Jack raised the book above his head. "There's no way I'm letting that THING anywhere near me!"

Smash gnashed his teeth and waved again. *Jingle-jingle-jingle* went the bells. He pointed toward the latch on the window and mimed opening it.

The professor adjusted his glasses and carefully got to his feet. He opened his desk drawer and started to shuffle around the contents, muttering, "I'm sure I have one here, they're great for bribing students — despite that ridiculous school policy. Aha, yes, here we go." Then he pulled something out and calmly walked over to the window.

Before Jack could react, the professor had opened the window and, with a burst of cold wind and a smattering of raindrops, the goblin catapulted himself through the open window. He landed neatly on the floor and started to sniff the air.

Jack's legs nearly gave way as he gasped, "YOU LET IT IN THE ROOM?" He scrambled backward, holding his book up like a shield.

"You see," the professor said, crouching down and facing the goblin, "Smash really isn't dangerous. He's just always craving sugar." He reached out to the creature and offered it the object in his hand — a bag of chocolate candies.

Jack watched in shock as the goblin politely tottered over and took the offered chocolate. "Oh," he said, slowly lowering the book.

Then Smash opened his mouth as wide as a bear-trap

and ripped into the plastic bag, eating it along with the half-melted chocolate.

"There." The professor wiped his hands together. "If you give him something sugary, then he's a very loyal friend. I'm guessing that taking away and eating the chocolate was Mr. Scrimp's unfortunate mistake — Smash really doesn't like to be teased."

The goblin growled in agreement and continued to rip into the chocolates.

"Uh-huh," Jack muttered. He gingerly put the book down on a nearby table, but he didn't take his eyes off the monster merrily stuffing its face on the floor.

The professor hummed and sat back down in his seat. "Now, where were we? Ah yes, we were talking about the fact that you — unfortunately — have been marked as Gretel's next victim."

He reached into his desk, pulled out several more packets of chocolate candies, and handed a couple to Jack. "Here you go. Think of them as dog treats."

Jack watched Smash eat and discovered that the goblin actually ate in a similar way to his dog — messily and with obvious joy. This made him relax slightly. Jack opened one of the packets of candy and sat back down in his seat. He gingerly popped one in his mouth, watching the goblin to make sure he wasn't going to suddenly jump on him and wrestle the candy from between his teeth.

The he realized what the professor had just said.

"Uh — hang on, I'm her *what*?"

The professor leaned back in his chair and laced his fingers together, making a steeple under his chin.

"Ah yes, we never did get to that part, did we? Too busy feeding our unexpected guest here. As I was saying, every generation Gretel gives away the jar to some poor child. Someone she is going to make an example of and punish. She gives it to her victims to terrify them before she casts her spell. It's a bit, well, flashy, but she does seem to like showing off her magic."

"So why do I have it?" Jack asked.

"Because, my dear boy, as I said, you are, unfortunately, her next victim."

Jack felt the chocolate in his mouth turn sour.

"Fairy tales are there to entertain children, but also to warn them." The professor sighed. "Every generation, there is another fairy tale, each different, but with the same process. First, Gretel gives away the jar to her next victim. When the jar is opened — and it always gets opened — she finds them and casts a spell on them that represents what she thinks is wrong with children of that generation. If she thinks children born in a certain time are all attention-seeking, she might turn one poor soul into a ghost, doomed to be ignored forever. Or if she thinks that one generation is all incredibly vain, she'll turn a pretty child into an ugly toad. Rapunzel, for example, was locked up in a tower forever because Gretel thought all children of that generation had ridiculous hairstyles. You have been given the cookie jar, so I'm afraid that you're next."

"Oh. Right." Jack digested this hideous thought for a moment. "Um, so what's my generation done?"

The professor shook his head. "I have no idea. Can you think of anything? I'm so out of touch with the youth of today."

Jack shrugged. At that moment, his phone gave a loud beep. Automatically he grabbed it and scrolled though his messages to make sure he hadn't missed anything important. Then he looked up to see the professor staring at him strangely.

"What?" Jack asked.

The professor pointed at his phone. "I can't be sure, but I would bet all the books in my library that Gretel has a punishment in mind that has something to do with the gadget in your hand. Young people don't talk to each other anymore; they just stare at their phones. She's from a time when that would be seen as extremely rude."

"What, ruder than casting spells on innocent children?" Jack snorted. But he gazed down at his phone with a new fear. Maybe he should cut back on his phone time for a bit, just in case.

Silence fell over the little study. Somewhere, a clock ticked. Even Smash was quiet, the chocolate finished. He watched the two humans with wide eyes.

"Well, how do I stop her?" Jack asked.

Another awkward silence. "I don't know."

"Great. No, really?"

"Really. No one has ever stopped her! Oh, some have avoided her evil plans, but they're rare. They tend to be special children — brave, generous, or good. And they've never managed to destroy her. She always comes back, stronger than ever."

Biting his lip, Jack realized he had no chance. Nobody had ever said he was particularly good at anything. He was just average and always had been.

Smash stood up and pattered over to Jack's chair. Jack flinched and quickly held out the last packet of candy. "Here you go — I don't want them anyway."

Smash blinked and, with a great effort, shook his head and sat down at Jack's feet. The goblin mimed eating, snapping his jaws together and rubbing his tummy, then gestured toward Jack.

"Uh, thanks," Jack said. "But honestly, you can have it. I suddenly feel a bit sick, you know, considering your evil sister has it in for me." He picked up the chocolates from his lap and gingerly tossed them at the goblin. Smash leaped into the air and grabbed the bag before biting down hard on the plastic wrapper. Chocolate candies exploded all over the carpet, and Jack nearly smiled — but then he stopped. He had just realized that very soon he could be turned into something as awful as a sugar-addicted goblin.

The professor leaned forward in his chair. "There could be a way! I've dedicated most of my life to researching the true origins of these fairy tales. After years of dead ends, I finally unearthed something that the villagers tried to keep buried because they were ashamed they ignored the white witch's warning." Looking around the room, as though checking that no one was listening, he whispered, "There's a prophecy about how to destroy Gretel! We'll probably just need to go on small quest to figure it out. . . ."

"A what?" Jack had had enough. Standing up from this chair, he shouted, "I don't want to hear any more! Witches, fairies, goblins, and now you want me to go on some sort of quest to figure out a prophecy? I'm going home, to my normal house to feed my, um, nearly normal cat!"

Smash burped and stood. "Smash gooooo weeeeeth Jaaaaack," he gurgled.

"No, you dumb goblin!" Jack shouted. "I'm going home, on my own, because I'm not having anything more to do with either of you!" He grabbed his bag and stomped across the room to the door.

Smash scowled and stomped his feet too. "Smash gooooo hooooome!" he howled. Then, as quick as a striking piranha, he leaped across the room and dove through the open window.

Jack gasped and ran over to the window. A fall from that height would kill anyone — but there was nothing outside. The goblin had vanished.

"Don't worry," the professor said, taking a sip of his tea. "He'll be fine. He always is. I've read all about it. He's turned up in every legend since Gretel started her evil work — and you wouldn't believe how many people have tried to kill him over the years! He's been drowned, boiled, set on fire, tarred, and feathered. Jumping from a second floor window isn't going to hurt him."

"Really? Oh. But still, I'm, you know, sorry," Jack mumbled to the cloudiness outside. With a sigh, he slung his bag over his shoulder and made his way to the door again. He ignored the professor's alarmed face and reached out for the handle.

The professor stood up, knocking his teacup to the floor. "You can't leave — not now! For the first time in over three hundred years, the victim realizes who the witch really is. Together we can stop her, for good!" He let his hands fall to his sides. "If you leave, I'm afraid that you won't survive for long."

Jack came to a halt, his hand curled around the door handle. If he walked out, he could just deny all knowledge of the cookie jar. Go home, keep a cross or something under his pillow, and try to forget this ever happened. Maybe she would leave him alone. This was the real world, after all, not some old and forgotten fairy tale.

He tightened his grip on the handle, but a nagging voice whispered in his head. What if she didn't leave him alone? Even if she did miraculously forget about him (and the odds, he thought, did not look good), what about the other children in the world she would target for the next four hundred years?

The school bell rang, interrupting his thoughts. Jack swallowed hard. He had made up his mind. He turned round and saw the professor's anxious face.

"OK," he said simply.

The professor grinned and pumped one fist into the air in triumph. "An excellent and, may I say, very wise decision."

Jack thought this was a good time to go — he'd learned all he could take for one day. The professor cried, "Come back tomorrow, same time! I'll try to find more about the prophecy tonight!" He frowned and turned around, staring at the vast piles of books covering every surface. "I'm sure it's in one of these books. . . ."

Jack opened the door and left the professor thumbing through an enormous leather-bound volume.

* * *

He spent the rest of the day in a haze of confusion. He listened with one ear to his friends' chatter as they tried to rationalize what had happened to their principal. The whole school was still buzzing with theories — nothing nearly this exciting had happened at their school for years, not since the sixth-graders had gone on strike to avoid extra PE — but Jack didn't join in.

At lunch Hannah tried to cheer Jack up by asking what Mr. Scrimp had looked like close up when he barfed all over the place. "Was it really disgusting?" she asked.

But Jack just shrugged and wandered off to sit down. He absentmindedly poured gravy all over his ice cream instead of hot fudge, while his friends exchanged concerned looks. As he spooned the lumps of gravy-covered ice cream into his mouth, all he could think about was what Gretel had planned for him. If he was lucky, he'd just throw up in front of the whole school as well. If he was unlucky . . . he didn't want to think about it.

At the end of the day, Jack walked home alone, and his thoughts turned back to the strange conversation he'd had with the professor. He wasn't sure what the professor could do to help. Maybe they were both destined to end up in a book of fairy tales, along with hundreds of other victims. *But,* he thought as he trudged along the dim streets, *it's nice to know I'm not alone.* He peered through the gloom, trying to see if he could spot a small figure with a jester hat. But there was nobody in sight. He could only hear the rattle of the wind.

He was blissfully unaware of what was waiting for him at home. . . .

CHAPTER 10
SMASH

Jack arrived home to chaos. As he neared his house, he could hear the TV blaring. That was normal. What wasn't normal were the gales of laughter coming from the front room. Jack thought his parents had given up laughing years ago, along with walking the dog and eating vegetables. He hurried to the front door and yanked it open. He inched his head around the front room door . . . and gasped.

Mr. and Mrs. Riddle were sitting on the sofa.

And squashed between them was Smash.

The little goblin was shoving handfuls of popcorn into his mouth. Jack's parents each held a bag of popcorn, and every time Smash reached a gnarled hand into a bag, they roared with laughter. Jack couldn't believe it. He'd thought the goblin had run away, but he must have figured out where he lived and gone straight there. But how? And why? Surely his parents realized that they were sitting with a monster — he wasn't exactly cuddly and fluffy. But they were treating Smash like some kind of adorable puppy. Were they under a magic spell? Suddenly Jack had a horrible thought. What if this was his aunt's spell — to make his parents love Smash more than they loved him? Or to make them think the goblin *was* him?

This last thought propelled Jack into the room, stumbling and tongue-tied. Mrs. Riddle looked up from the goblin wedged between them and grinned. "Jack! Hello, love! How was school?"

Wondering if it was some sort of trick, Jack edged toward a chair on the other side of the room. Never taking his eyes off the weird scene in front of him, he sat down carefully, as though the chair was a bomb.

"We've been having a great time with this little lovey!" his mom explained.

Both parents turned back to the goblin and gazed at it. Smash continued to guzzle from the bags, spraying crumbs and spit all over his feet. They smiled indulgently.

Jack opened his mouth to say something, but only a croak came out. He cleared his throat and whispered, "Uh . . . the 'little lovey'?"

His parents said together, "The monkey!"

Jack nearly burst out laughing but managed to change it into a cough at the last minute.

Mr. Riddle ignored Jack and said with pride, "I've always wanted one of these. They're really intelligent, you know. He would make a great family pet."

His mom started to tickle the "monkey" under his chin. Jack wondered if he would bite off her fingers, but, to his amazement, a silly look spread over Smash's face. Jack could have sworn it was happiness.

"Well, where's he going to sleep?" Jack demanded.

His parents were stumped for a second, then his dad declared, "He'll sleep with you. We can put a basket at the bottom of your bed. The dog can sleep outside. Do the wimpy mutt some good, if you ask me."

Mrs. Riddle gushed over Smash, calling him her "wittle sausage." He nosed her hand, obviously asking for more pats on the head — or more food.

The white cat chose this moment to saunter into the room. Jack leaned over and scooped her up. Then the cat and Smash spotted each other.

Both began to howl.

The cat wriggled, scratched, and hissed in Jack's arms. Smash jumped over the back of the sofa, taking a bag of popcorn with him.

"Get that crazy cat out of here!" Mr. Riddle yelled.

Jack tightened his grip on the cat and made for the door.

Mrs. Riddle had disappeared behind the sofa and was cooing in a gooey voice, "There, there, little monkey, don't let that nasty kitty bother you. Have some chocolate."

Crunching sounds followed Jack out the room. He decided that Smash wasn't going to hurt his parents — not when they were feeding him so well. Feeling relieved for the time being, he fled to his bedroom.

Sitting down on his messy bed, Jack placed the cat in front of him. "Now listen, you," he scolded, "stop acting up! I've already got enough problems without you causing a scene all the time."

She hissed as if she understood. The hairs on Jack's neck stood up. She always seemed to understand him — and normal animals just didn't do that. There was something unnatural about her.

She sprang back up and sat on the pillows, next to his head, purring like an expensive car engine.

Mr. Riddle knocked on Jack's door. Without waiting for an answer, he walked in carrying a basket. Smash peeked over the edge of the rim. All Jack could see were two tarnished bells and a pair of blackberry eyes.

His father hesitated. "That cat isn't going to do anything silly, is it?" he asked.

Jack shrugged. He had been worried that the cat would pounce on the basket, but she seemed to have made her point. She started to wash her paws with a very pink tongue, ignoring the drooling goblin.

Mr. Riddle nodded and put the basket down gently. Jack felt a sting of jealousy as he saw how careful his father was being with the goblin.

Mr. Riddle grunted a good night to Jack, patted the cat, and threw a candy cane at Smash.

Jack stared at the goblin, who grinned back.

"Smaaaassshhh hooommme," he gurgled.

Groaning, Jack switched off the light and decided to call it a day. Like it or not, he was stuck with a goblin boy and a (probably) magical cat. That was enough for the time being. Anything else would just have to wait until morning.

* * *

BBRRRRRIIIIINNG! BBRRRRRIIIIINNG!

Jack rolled over and slapped the alarm clock to silence it.

Yawning, he sat up and peered into the dark room, then jumped when a huge pair of green eyes stared at him from the end of the bed.

"Cat," he groaned. He realized he was going to have to give her a name soon. He couldn't just keep calling her "cat."

Muttering about how he had never tasted cat soup and how delicious she might be in a pot (Jack really wasn't at his best in the mornings), he flung back the covers and swung his feet to the floor.

Remembering Smash, he peered at the basket. There he was, snoring happily. The goblin's face was covered in dried chocolate, and his hands and feet were dangling over the edges of the basket.

Jack shuddered and decided not to wake him. He hoped that the goblin would simply doze the day away, so Jack didn't have to worry about what he was up to.

Still yawning, he shuffled into the bathroom. The cat stayed at the end of the bed, flicking her tail back and forth and watching the goblin snore.

While Jack was brushing his teeth, he had an idea. He really wanted a second opinion on the cat. Was she just freakishly clever? Or was she magic? If he took her to school and asked the professor, he might be able to tell him.

He frowned. How was he supposed to smuggle her in? The teachers would all be wary of animals in school after what had happened to the principal yesterday.

Jack felt a twinge of guilt and wondered if Mr. Scrimp was OK. The principal had been taken to the hospital after his awful encounter with Smash, and no one knew how long he would be there for. Apparently he was just sitting, staring at the wall, muttering about Mars bars and mad monkeys.

Jack finished brushing his teeth and went back to his room to get dressed. But before he did, he chucked the cat into the hall — just in case she wasn't a normal animal. After the week he had been through, nothing was impossible anymore.

Then he staggered downstairs into the kitchen where his mom was making a big breakfast. The smell of sizzling bacon was fantastic.

Mrs. Riddle had a bacon sandwich with a side of scrambled eggs for breakfast every day. She claimed she needed to eat a good breakfast if she was going to stay on her feet at the hospital for hours on end. She was a plump woman with soft blue eyes and pudgy hands. She gestured toward the pan, but Jack shook his head. Despite the wonderful aroma of bacon, he was too nervous to eat much. He sat down to pick at a small bowl of cereal.

Mrs. Riddle hummed as she cracked the eggs into a pan with butter and salt. She smiled at Jack and said, "Well! How are you this morning? Feeling better? How's that dear little monkey?"

"Um, I'm good, and the monkey is asleep," Jack mumbled.

"What do you want to call it?"

"Who? Smash?"

"Smash! That's a great name! I did notice that he made a noise very like the word 'smash.' I could've almost sworn he was talking!"

Jack gave her a patient smile and replied, "Wow, who would've thought it?"

Mrs. Riddle smiled and tossed the scrambled eggs onto a plate with the crispy bacon. Timmy whined outside and scratched at the door to be let in. Jack took pity on the poor dog and opened it. Timmy bounded in and skidded to a halt underneath the cooker.

Rolling her eyes and tutting, Mrs. Riddle picked up a piece of burnt bacon and dropped it at Timmy's paws. The dog wolfed it down whole then looked up again, wanting more. She ignored him and sat down to eat.

Mr. Riddle strode through the kitchen, grabbed a yogurt from the fridge, plonked himself down next to Jack, and tore the lid from his container.

"So . . . looking forward to school today?"

Jack nodded.

"The monkey still alive?" he asked with a teasing smile.

Jack nodded again.

"Humph. Well, it'll be a nice family pet once you get used to it. Give you a bit of company in the evenings, instead of always staring at your phone."

Jack started to smile. It had been a while since his dad had joked around with him. But then Mr. Riddle frowned. He spooned his breakfast into his mouth and thought about how he'd try to ask for some more hours at work this week. If they didn't give him any, he was going to have to dip into the savings again. He stared at his son as he chewed, his mind far away.

But Jack only saw the frown. "Whatever," he grouched, pushing his cereal round the bowl.

Mr. Riddle sighed and scooped up the last of his yogurt before getting up and throwing the empty carton in the recycling.

Jack quickly finished his cereal, patted Timmy on the head, and went to fetch his school bag. His usual morning ritual — except this time he was going to smuggle a cat to school.

And he couldn't just let her sit on his shoulder like she usually did.

He started up the stairs to his room, thinking about the best way to do it. After considering, and discarding, several daring plans involving catapults and flying cats, he decided the only way was the simplest — he would just have to zip her in his schoolbag. And hope she stayed quiet.

CHAPTER 11
THE PROPHECY

Twenty minutes later Jack was struggling to stay calm. He was walking toward the school gates and trying to keep hold of his bag, which was difficult when it was jumping around in his arms, as his furious cat hissed and spat inside. Clamping the bundle close to his chest, he hurried through the school gates and into the building, hoping no one would see him. But then a paw tipped with sharp claws burst through the bag's fabric and started to swipe at the air. Jack walked faster, shoving the paw back into the bag, gripping the handle with white-knuckled hands.

"Jack!" a voice called out. Ayo popped his head around their homeroom door. "What're you doing? Why're you not in homeroom?"

Jack tried to wave, but nearly lost his grip on the bag. He quickened his pace, feeling the cat's fury as she tried to catapult out of the small hole she had made.

Ayo frowned and wrinkled his nose to push his glasses back up. "You'll get a detention if you're not careful. You coming out after school on Friday? We're all going to go down to the park for a bit."

At that moment the professor came running down the corridor, shaking a piece of parchment. "Jack!" he cried. "I've found it! I've found the information we need!"

Ayo stared in bewilderment.

Jack shrugged and tapped the side of his head. "It's that batty history teacher."

Narrowing his eyes, Ayo was about to answer when their homeroom teacher's voice boomed out from the open classroom. "Ayotomiwa! What are you doing by the door? We still have the announcements to read through! Come back in and close the door behind you."

With a suspicious look, Ayo's head disappeared behind the door, which swung shut after him.

At that moment Jack lost his grip on the bag. It went bouncing down the hall toward the professor. Jack raced after it.

"Stop, you stupid cat!" he hissed as he hurried down the hall past the full classrooms. He managed to pounce on the bag and picked it up firmly. "Behave!"

The professor reached Jack and waved the piece of parchment under his nose. "I found it! I found the prophecy in an old manuscript. I knew I wouldn't sleep a wink last night, so I stayed here and tried to find it. And I did! It's our first clue about how we can stop the witch!"

Jack heard a giggle behind him. He swung around to see two girls gawking at him and the professor. He realized how insane the professor sounded.

"That's great, but, um, can you tell me later?" he asked. "I'm already late for homeroom. I can't have another tardy, or I'll get detention."

The professor blinked, as if he had just remembered they were in school. "Ah yes, of course! Don't worry, I'll sign you in later. Come on, m'boy, this is far more important than school — and I *never* thought I'd say that. Walk with me." He strode off down the hall, and Jack hurried to keep up, trying to keep a grip on his squirming bag.

They walked past classrooms full of students, their bright chatter floating through the thin walls and down the hallway. While they walked, the professor smoothed out the piece of yellow parchment in his hands. "Here it is!" he cried. Jack winced. The professor really didn't get how to talk quietly. "The town mayor's diary."

Despite his embarrassment, Jack stared at it with interest. The parchment was brittle and looked as though it was about to fall apart.

The professor peered at the tiny, cramped handwriting and read, "'The witch stood on the gallows and spoke the following words:

"'*First comes the goblin, then the witch. Destruction will rain down on thy children's heads. It will always be thus for several hundred years, unless water and spirit bring fire to the place where earth and air meet.'*

"'To our eternal shame, we hanged her before she could explain what her words meant. And now our cursed children will suffer for our terrible sins.'"

The professor glanced eagerly at Jack's blank face. "Fascinating stuff, isn't it? The town mayor felt dreadful about the hanging and wrote it all down. It didn't stop him from getting rid of his wife the same way, though. He had her hanged in 1615 — apparently he grinned the whole way through. He soon changed his tune when her ghost came back to haunt him. She clanged pots over his head all night long! He never got another wink of sleep again, poor man. Went quite insane."

By now they had done one lap around the first-floor halls. A few students had noticed them and nudged each other as Jack and the professor walked past the classrooms. Jack's ears burned as he knew what they would be saying — *teacher's pet.* It didn't help that his bag was also still wriggling around in his arms, making it look as though he was doing a funny dance as he walked.

He realized that the professor had asked him a question. He said, "Sorry, what was that?"

"I said, what happened at your aunt's house? I need to hear the whole story — leave out no detail. It could help us understand how to fulfill the prophecy and stop Gretel."

With a gulp Jack remembered he had bigger things to worry about than being seen as the teacher's pet. As they did another lap through the halls, Jack told the professor about following his aunt into the woods and seeing the carousel cauldron. When Jack told him about his aunt's extra head under the hat, the professor grinned.

"Cause and effect, Jack. Yes, she can make herself look young. It's called *glamour magic*. But her evil nature has to go somewhere. You can't be so evil and not have it show up eventually. That extra head is her *real* one; she simply put a spell on it and gave herself a new head underneath." He grimaced. "Gosh, that must've hurt! But witches can't go around looking like terrifying old hags. Children would run screaming away from them, and then how would they cast their spells?"

They reached Jack's homeroom door again and paused outside it. His bag was suspiciously still. Jack wasn't sure why. Was the cat exhausted, or just plotting her next move?

"What about the other women on the carousel cauldron things?" Jack asked. "Who were they?"

The professor shuddered. "They must've been witches from other countries — luckily for us, they were probably just visiting. Sounds like you stumbled on a coven meeting, where all the witches from around the globe meet in one place for one evening. Probably why she didn't smell you immediately. She was distracted by her guests. They meet once a year and decide on all the horrible spells they're going to cast on children all over the world. You were very, very lucky to leave that forest alive."

Jack had just opened his mouth to explain about how the white cat had helped him escape (and that she was currently shredding his school bag to pieces), when there was a loud buzzing: the bell for first hour.

Doors burst open and students streamed around them, tapping away on their phones. They looked like zombies as they walked with their heads down, shuffling to their next classes. Teachers called out threatening punishments about what would happen if the students didn't put their phones away immediately but were ignored by most students.

At that moment, Jack's bag leaped out of his arms and started hopping across the floor. He dove after it, but nearly collided with a group of older kids, who growled, "Watch where you're going!"

The professor was totally oblivious to both the crowd of students and the escaping bag.

"Don't worry about a thing!" he cried, waving the parchment above his head. "We'll beat the witch or die trying!"

Jack crawled along the floor, trying to avoid all the feet. "Sorry, sorry, sorry."

Bounce, bounce, boing, went the bag.

The students started to thin out as they moved toward their first class. Jack could see a clear path to his bag. He pounced on it and stood up, breathing heavily.

"Oops!" The professor slapped his hand over his mouth.

"I'm supposed to be teaching. Ugh, the thought of having to teach history to a roomful of bored teenagers when I could be cracking this prophecy! Drat. I'll have to see you at break. By the way, what's wrong with your bag? It's trying to run away!"

The professor stomped off, cursing under his breath.

Opening the bag, Jack ducked to avoid the paw trying to scratch his face. "Stay still, or I'll dump you back in that creepy forest," he hissed. The cat mewled angrily, but stopped jumping around. Relieved, Jack turned toward his first classroom.

Taking a deep breath, he leaned against the wall for a several seconds before going into the class. The minute he walked in, he knew everyone would stare at him. He wanted to at least look like he hadn't spent the last few minutes battling a wild cat. He closed his eyes and, to his horror, felt a familiar dizzy feeling wash over him. The last time he had felt this way, he'd been running from an eerie mist in the place his aunt had called the Lost Forest.

Oh no! he thought. His eyes flew open and flashing lights danced in front of his face. He reached out to the wall for balance, but his couldn't move his hands.

I can't faint — not at school — I'll never live it down!

Jack staggered away from the wall in an attempt to snap out of it. But it was too late. The flashing lights spread, and he fell unconscious to the floor.

CHAPTER 12

THE WHITE WITCH

Jack was dreaming. He knew he must be, because he could see his body on the floor, pale and still. He seemed to be floating above it.

A group of concerned students milled around his body, taking turns prodding him with their feet. They were the usual stragglers who used any excuse to be late for class — and today they had a great one.

Jack knew he should try to wake up, but it felt quite nice just floating in the air.

Huh, he thought, *so this is what flying feels like. Or maybe this is what dying feels like.*

He rolled over in the air and saw that where the ceiling should be, there was a tunnel of light. He floated toward it and could see tree branches waving in the wind at the end of the tunnel. The branches were huge and twisted, more like skeletons than trees. There was a sickly blue moon hanging in the sky.

Oh no, he thought in panic. *I'm heading back to the Lost Forest!* It was like a nightmare that he couldn't wake up from.

Hastily, he tried to turn and float back the other way. But some kind of force was pulling him along. He struggled to hold himself back by grabbing at the edges of the tunnel and was horrified when his hands clutched empty air.

The force increased, and Jack found himself rolling forward.

"Argh!" he shouted as he tumbled through the air. Hands flailing, he landed with a thud on the forest floor.

He groaned. Shaking his head, he pulled himself to his feet, wiping the mud off his jeans. Warily, he looked around.

Strange creatures surrounded him. Tiny balls of light darted around his head, squeaking in a flute-like language. A horse neighed to his right, and he turned his head to catch a glimpse of something shimmering, but it disappeared into the trees. All he saw before it vanished was a flicker of hooves and wings.

"Wait!" Jack cried. He was fascinated. Eyes wide in wonder, he raced over the soft, mossy ground to try to follow the horse.

He ran, but no matter how fast he went, the horse always stayed just out of his sight. His heart thudding, he finally reached a small glade. He realized he knew this place. Last time, there had been a nightmarish carousel stirring a foul mixture in a cauldron. But now, standing in the middle of the glade, there was only a woman in a velvet cloak the color of emeralds. Under the cloak she wore a glittering white dress, and her feet were encased in shimmering green glass slippers. Her face was hidden by the cloak's hood. Wisps of white hair floated out from underneath it. She stood absolutely still.

For some reason Jack wasn't afraid. The forest felt as though it was singing a lullaby that only he could hear, soothing away all his fears. Stepping toward the woman, he heard a clear voice like chiming bells and wolf song in his head.

"That's close enough, my young one. I am sorry for alarming thee, but this is the only way that we can meet. Dost thee comprehend why I have summoned thee?"

Jack hesitated. "Uh, no, not really."

There was a pause.

The woman spoke again, but this time there was a frown in her voice. "But thou ist nearly ready to understand and fulfill the prophecy?"

Jack hesitated. "Not exactly . . ."

"Oh, for pity's sake." The woman threw back her hood. "Must I do EVERYTHING?"

He gaped at her. The dreamy feeling disappeared, as if someone had flung a glass of cold water in his face. "What d'you mean?"

She put her hands on her hips. Now that he was closer to her, he could see that she had fine features and lashings of black lipstick. "Every time that dratted jar is opened, everyone expects me to know all the answers! What is wrong with people thinking for thyselves?"

Stung, Jack replied, "All I said was that I don't get it!"

The woman ignored him. "Me, me, me! That is all I hear from the endless parade of people who needest my help." Her fair hair whipped around her head as she walked over to a small boulder and sat down on it. "And these glass shoes pinch my feet," she moaned, reaching down to ease them off. "Ah, that is better! Girls these days have the right idea when it comes to sensible footwear. Sneakers are indeed the way forward. I never did like the whole 'professional dress' part of the job either." She put her fingers in the air and mimed quote marks, the modern gesture a startling contrast to her outfit. "Why is it that I cannot just wear a nice pair of woolen trousers, like thy twenty-first-century womenfolk? This outfit is deathly uncomfortable."

Then she glanced over at him and smiled with sympathy. "Yes, I know. Thou hast a raw deal, being the next victim and all. I just wish that people would finally work things out for themselves. Then I can stay blissfully dead and stop haunting these chilly dream realms in a steel corset." She patted the boulder in front of her with a very white hand. "Come on, then — take a seat. Let us see if I can drop enough hints for thee to figure out what to do next, hmm?"

"OK," Jack said slowly, making his way over the boulder. Warily, he sat down opposite her.

"Now," she said, "I can only come to meet thee three times —"

"Why's that?" Jack interrupted.

The woman opened her mouth, but nothing came out. She frowned and said, "It is just the rules! Honestly, dost thou not knowest anything about fairy tales?"

"Umm, not really."

She blinked several times in astonishment. "My, my, I can see why my sister in darkness chose thee as her next victim . . ."

"Why'd you mean?" Jack said defensively.

Holding her hands up, the woman replied, "No offense. Just observing. I do not have much else to do these days. Such a shame — thou seemest to be a nice young man. Anyway, as I said, I can only see thee three times — and this meeting counts." She ticked off her points as she spoke. "I am also not allowed to say what thou needest to know to understand how to fulfill the prophecy. The villagers killed me before I could explain my words. Because of this foolish act, I cannot tell thee what to do — thou hast to work it out on thy own. But there is nothing in the rules to say I can't give a few big hints."

"Oh! *You're* the white witch!" Jack exclaimed.

The woman closed her eyes for a minute as if in pain. "I think I am getting a headache. Yes, well done, I am a white witch." She gestured to her shimmering outfit. "What gavest me away?" she asked sarcastically.

Nodding eagerly, Jack leaned forward. "Yep, I get that, but I mean you're the one from the story. The professor told me about you! Didn't Gretel frame you for trying to cook and eat her brother? And, you know, get the villagers to —" He mimed a rope being strung round his neck, sticking his tongue out and gasping.

The white witch stood up and started to pace. Her cloak whirled around her bare feet as she walked. "Yes, and thanks to thee for reminding me! I am forced to haunt these woods while that pretender Gretel waltzes around with my wand." She folded her arms. "I should have just died and let myself rest in peace. But that would not be 'ethical,' would it?" she asked, using air quotes again. "So here we are, centuries later, and I am *still* waiting for some clever child to fulfill the prophecy. I really think I am due a rest after several hundred years. Dost thou agree?"

"Uh, right. So, what was this big hint you were going to tell me?"

She tilted her head to one side, and a small frown creased her perfect forehead. "Thou ist not very respectful," she sighed. "Usually the children are trembling at my feet by this point. Perhaps it would help if I got into character a bit more, yes?" She clapped her hands, and the light around her grew brighter.

Jack stared as the white witch seemed to catch fire. Flames flickered around her body, and her eyes turned pure white. He stood up and backed away from the rising heat of the dancing flames.

The white witch turned her blank eyes toward him and said in a voice like howling wolves, "Go and seek out the mermaid's sisters. They will tell thee what thou needest to know. Take the professor — he is a wise man. But be careful. The mermaids are ancient and dangerous."

Jack frowned. Where was he supposed to find a mermaid?

Perhaps he was meant to say something, because the white witch paused and said in a normal voice, "Dost thou get the hint?"

"Ummmmm. Nooo . . ."

She pulled a pained expression. "Really? The mention of mermaids did not give thee any ideas? Surely thou hast heard of the little mermaid?"

"Oh." Jack grinned, delighted he knew this one. "Yep, the Disney movie."

"No!" she shouted, slapping her head with one hand. Then she grumbled, "Talking to thee is far too much hard work. Until next time!"

He wanted to ask more questions, but the wind began to rise in the glade, making the leaves on the ground float and flutter. The white witch's cloak swirled in the breeze, whipping the hood from side to side. Jack strained to see her face within the flames, but he could only see a dim outline of her black lipstick. He realized her body was fading and he could see the trees through her.

With a scream of hot air, the figure in the glade faded away completely, and Jack was left alone. He shivered, suddenly realizing that the wind was whistling through the forest. It bit through his thin shirt and sweater, making him tremble with cold.

The wind stung his eyes so he had to squint. When he opened them fully again, he screamed, "Baaaagh!"

Standing in front of him, barely three inches away, was Gretel. She was smiling, but it wasn't a nice smile. It was terrifying. She stood totally still, not moving a muscle.

Jack took a quick step back. *One more,* he thought, *just one more step, then I can turn and run.* Little by little, he inched away from her. Just as he was steeling himself to take a final step, she said, "My, what big eyes you have."

Then a voice from under her hat rasped, "All the better to see me when I GOBBLE you up!"

Jack turned and ran faster than he had ever run in his life.

He heard her laughter behind him. "Remember, Jack," she said, her words floating on the wind, "I'm watching you! And very soon, when I cast my spell, that's all *you* will be able to do!"

What does that *mean?* he thought. *Please wake up, please wake up!*

* * *

SPLOSH!

He woke up on the floor of the school hallway, choking and dripping wet. A concerned ninth grader stared down at him and asked, "Are you all right?" Tall and stout, she looked like a born girl scout leader. At that moment, Jack thought she was the most beautiful girl he had ever seen.

She held out a hand and easily yanked Jack to his feet.

"Sorry about the water, but I saw you passed out on the floor and thought an ice-cold glass of water in the face was the fastest remedy!"

Jack stood on tiptoe and surprised her by giving her a huge hug and a loud kiss on the cheek.

"That's the best idea you've ever had! No, really, you're just fantastic!"

A bemused smile spread over her wide face. "Yes, well," she said gruffly, "you'd better get to class."

Jack grabbed his bag and scuttled off to his geography class. He stammered an excuse about being ill to the teacher and sat down. Shoving his bag under the desk, he spent the rest of the class with his head resting on his hands — and one foot firmly on the bag strap to stop it from running away.

Jack thought about the white witch's words. He counted down the minutes until break. Somehow, he and the professor had to figure out how to find some mermaids — and what they had to do with the prophecy. And all before the world's most evil witch decided on her favorite way to torture him for eternity.

With a groan, Jack let his head thump down onto the desk, ignoring the curious stares of the other students.

CHAPTER 13
THE MERMAIDS' TALE

Jack jumped up from his seat when the bell rang for break. His friends called out to ask him to join a game of football on the field. He said he'd be down in a minute, but turned toward the professor's office instead. Before Jack had time to knock on the door, a hand shot out and yanked him into the room by his collar.

"Good, you're here!" the professor beamed, letting go of his collar. "I've been trying to find something that will help us, but no luck so far."

Jack walked past him into the room and slung his bag on the floor. It started to squirm as the cat tried to get out.

"I couldn't find a thing, and I can't help thinking we're missing some vital clue! By the way, I think you need a new bag. It's trying to run away again."

Jack glanced down and saw his bag flopping across the floor. "I tried to tell you earlier. It's my new stupid cat!"

"Oh, that makes much more sense. But why did you bring it to school? I'm sure it's a very nice cat, but . . ."

Jack pounced on the bag and wrestled with the strap, trying to open it as quickly as possible. "I needed to ask you about it. I don't think it's normal."

Bounce, boing, bounce, went the bag.

"It followed me back from the glade where I saw Gretel on the carousel cauldron thing. Gretel called it the Lost Forest. Well, the white witch — I just spoke to her actually, think she made me faint or something so she could talk to me, really weird feeling. She hates the fact that she has to haunt the woods. I think she'd rather be dead actually, she told me that this morning. You know, the woman that Gretel got the villagers to kill, so —"

"Wait!" The professor cried, staring in fascination. "Start from the beginning. You found a cat in the forest. Then you spoke to the white witch this morning — how did that happen? She is technically supposed to be dead!"

Jack took a big breath and explained what had happened to him, all while trying to untie his bag. After he had finished, he finally managed to free the cat from his bag. She tumbled out in a ball of fur, fangs, and claws. Hissing and spitting, she slashed Jack across the nose with one paw.

"Ouch! Stop it! Don't you think I've got enough problems without a bleeding nose too?"

Jack nursed his injury and glared at the cat.

The professor's eyes grew wide. "She told you to speak

to the mermaids, you say. I wonder. I just wonder . . ." He clambered to his feet and started rummaging around in his desk.

"Aha!" In his hand was a battered mirror, the kind you find on a dressing table.

"Is it a magic mirror? Can it tell the future, or, I dunno, show us dinosaurs or something?" Jack asked eagerly. He was expecting something fantastic and magical after that build-up.

But the professor just eyed him strangely and said, "What? Oh no, it's just an old mirror."

The professor held the mirror in front of the cat, with a look of adoration. "Look . . . ," he breathed. "Look at her reflection!"

Sighing, Jack decided to humor the professor and look . . . and then fell back with a shout of surprise. Instead of a cat in the mirror, there was a young girl . . . with the body of a fish.

"Yes!" the professor breathed. "At last, I've seen a legend of the sea!" He regarded Jack with shining eyes. "Jack," he said, "this is Ariel."

"Uh, who?"

"That, young man, is what the ancients called a drowned god."

"Nope, still don't get it."

"A mermaid! A real one, straight from a legend." The professor seemed so thrilled, he was nearly in tears. "In all my research, I never dreamed I would see such a thing. And you've made it possible!"

Jack stared at the reflection in the mirror. He had always thought mermaids looked exactly like a half human, half fish. This one was different. She had long, flowing hair the color of seaweed, and gray eyes with no pupils. Her skin was covered with dull silver scales and her long hands were webbed and tipped with razor-sharp nails. But oddest of all was her nose. It was missing. Instead, she had two small holes in the middle of her face. She smiled suddenly, showing four rows of teeth. It made her look like a baby shark.

Jack gulped and inched even farther away from the mirror. "But why is she, er, a mermaid in the mirror and a cat now?"

"Oh, it's because she was enchanted by the witch! You see, this is the *real* little mermaid. You've heard the story?"

Jack blinked. "Yes, the lovey-dovey one."

The professor watched Jack with narrowed eyes. "This isn't a story with a happy ending. You can forget the modern version. This is the real story — and it's far too dark for most children to hear."

Reverently, the professor picked up Ariel and placed her in his armchair. She watched him as he began the story.

"Mermaids live in the deepest, darkest, coldest parts of the oceans."

Jack snorted. "Huh! I think we would've noticed them!" he said, folding his arms.

"Really. Are you aware that only two percent of the sea has been explored? And that we know more about what's in *space* than we do about what lives at the bottom of the sea?"

Uncertainly, Jack shook his head.

"It's true," said the professor firmly. "Long ago, when apes were just about to evolve into humans, some apes decided to live in the sea. They evolved to swim in water, and we evolved to walk on the earth. Over the years, they sank farther and farther beneath the waves, until they became forgotten. Only old tales of mysterious people, with the fins and tail of a fish, survived to be told by the fire on a dark winter's night. Until one day a mermaid fell in love with a land-ape." He smiled. "That's a human."

Jack blushed and felt bad about snorting before. It actually did sound kind of believable. Well, the evolving part. He wasn't so sure about the love bit. *Yuck.*

The professor said, "Well, the little mermaid — that's Ariel here — liked to swim up from the inky depths of the sea and feel the sunlight on her scales. She would sing to the sea birds, and the sweetness of her voice calmed the wind. One wild and stormy night, she was playing in the crashing waves and saw a ship being pulled apart in the storm. Humans were dying in the cold sea. Normally, she would ignore them — what were land-apes to her? But she saw a handsome prince and instantly fell in love. She saved him from the deadly water and pulled him to the shore."

Ariel sighed and rested her head on her paws.

The professor smiled grimly. "But she belonged in the deep ocean, and he could only survive on land. She knew she couldn't stay with the prince. So she struck a deal with the sea witch — that's Gretel to you and me."

At the sound of Gretel's name, Ariel began to hiss softly.

"The witch gave her legs — but only in exchange for the mermaid's beautiful singing voice. She also had to persuade the prince to marry her by the next full moon, or the sea witch would own the mermaid's soul."

Jack shuddered. Gretel didn't come across well in any of these stories. He tuned in to the professor's story again.

"Well, as you probably know, the little mermaid could only follow the prince and smile at him, because she had sold her voice for legs. Sadly, he became betrothed to a beautiful princess, and the little mermaid knew she had failed. The night before the royal wedding, she cried silently into the sea, missing her old home and friends. But then her three sisters came to the surface and held out a knife with a pearl handle and a steel blade. They all had shaved heads.

"'Take it,' they cried. 'We sold our hair to the sea witch for the knife. If you kill the prince with the knife by full moon tonight, you will be free.' But the little mermaid still loved the prince. She went and sat by his bed while he slept that night. She wept and raised the knife, but she couldn't kill him. And when the morning came, she was gone. The sea witch had claimed her soul.

"Legend tells us that she was turned into seafoam, but the witch gave her a worse fate. Gretel turned her into an animal that can only survive on land and loathes water. An animal with a singing voice so horrible, it sings only at night. A cat."

Ariel let out a yowl at the end of the story, pointing her nose at the ceiling. Jack winced. *Yeah,* he thought, *not the nicest sound in the world.*

"OK. So, I've got Smash at my house, who is really Hansel. He was given to me by the witch Gretel to tell me I'm her next victim. She does this to all her victims — kind of a 'look what I can do, and you're next,' right?"

The professor smiled and nodded, pushing his glasses up his nose.

Jack plowed on. "And I've also got a cat that used to be the little mermaid. So what do we do?"

The professor got to his feet and gestured with the mirror toward the cat. "Now we go on an emergency field trip!"

There was a pause while Jack digested this. "Right. A field trip. Uh, where?"

The professor blinked and lowered the mirror. "Why, Scotland, of course." He glanced at his watch. "Goodness, I must update my health records at once, otherwise the school will never let us go by tomorrow morning." He yanked open the door and ran from the room, shouting over his shoulder, "I'll drop the forms off with your homeroom teacher at the end of the day! And bring a warm coat! It's chilly where we're going!"

"OK," Jack replied. "Again, why Scotland? Professor!"

Jack stood and watched the professor run down the hall, feeling slightly stunned.

"Mad goblins, wicked witches, dangerous mermaids, and

now a school field trip," he grumbled. "Lucky me."

* * *

The next morning, Jack was sitting in a train car and trying to doze off. But every few seconds he was jerked awake by the clacking of the train as it trundled through the countryside. He rubbed his eyes and tried to clear his fuzzy head, remembering that they were headed for the seaside town of Glenselkie, famous for its crumbling castle and cold weather.

At least, he thought, *I'm getting a day off school. Even if it is to hunt down a load of mythical monsters, that's better than math.* Jack had arrived home last night armed with a note from the professor explaining that Jack had been chosen to attend an emergency field trip to visit the castle in Glenselkie because of his "excellent aptitude for history." Jack had been quite excited to show his parents such a gushing note about his history work.

But Mr. Riddle had narrowed his eyes at the mention of an all-day school trip. "As long as it's just the one day off!" he said. "You shouldn't be wasting your time on subjects you'll probably drop in a few years anyway. History won't get you anywhere in life."

Mrs. Riddle frowned at her husband and patted Jack reassuringly on the shoulder. "Of course you can go. I'll drop you off at the station in the morning."

Jack thought his mom and dad were going to argue about the trip, but luckily they were more interested in telling him all about Smash.

They called Smash "their strange new pet." Mrs. Riddle

watched the daytime talk shows with the goblin, and they sat together on the sofa munching chocolates all day. Both seemed extremely happy.

When Jack had gotten up that morning, rubbing his eyes with exhaustion, he had offered to put Ariel in his schoolbag. He thought she would want to go along, but she sat in the corner of his room with her back to him, tail twitching.

"Come on, Ariel," he'd said. "Don't you want to go on a trip?" But the cat had refused to budge. With a shrug, Jack had left her there and clattered out of the house to catch his train. His mom had given him a ride, yawning in the dawn light, and made him promise to call her when he got back in the evening so she could pick him up.

The train had pulled up just as they rounded the corner to the station. Jack raced out of the car, throwing a hasty goodbye over his shoulder, then jumped into the train car just before the doors closed. He found the professor already snoring away at a corner table at the front. Jack had settled down to try to sleep himself.

A jolt made the passengers all jump in their seats. The professor gave a rasping snore like a dying chain saw, then opened his eyes. He stretched and smiled. "I do so love traveling by train! And I'm very fond of Scotland — what a treat."

Jack crossed his arms and said, "Great, you're awake. You can tell me why we're going to Glenselkie."

"Oh, did I not say? Whoops. It's where the mermaids live, of course. The Scots have always known about them, and they've found a way to make sure they're kept happy." He shook his head. "Scottish sailors really have a hard time, what with the terrible weather. And if that wasn't bad enough, they have to deal with those creatures too. They've come to a sort of peace, but if the mermaids don't get a share of the fish they catch, they have a nasty tendency to sink the fishermen's boats. Where do you think the Loch Ness monster myths come from?"

"Um, tourists and fake photos?"

"Wrong!" Looking gleeful, the professor reached under the table and pulled out a book from his bag. It had a picture of the Loch Ness monster on the front, but the monster had the shadow of a mermaid. "I wrote a radical book about the subject." His face darkened. "Unfortunately, my university colleagues didn't agree. Thought I was insane! Laughed at me everywhere I went! Then they took my funding away and fired me."

"Can't you go and work for another one?"

"I've been fired from six universities. No one will hire me now, only middle schools." Nearly on the verge of tears, the professor took a deep breath. "But we'll show 'em, eh?"

Jack nodded, feeling uncomfortable. He quickly thought of something to change the subject. "Ariel didn't want to come with us today. You'd think she'd want to see her family again."

"Really? Hmm." Reaching into his bag again, the professor pulled out his plaid thermos of tea and two china cups. He carefully poured himself a cup and then offered one to Jack, who took the steaming brew to warm his hands. "I suspect she doesn't want her sisters to see her. It is a huge insult for a mermaid to be turned into a land animal. They can be a bit snobby about that sort of thing."

Jack took a sip of tea and wondered which animal he would hate to be turned into the most. A snotty slug? Or a big, hairy sewer rat? *Yuck*, he thought. *Definitely a rat.* He shuddered and wrapped his hands more tightly round the cup. Not for the first time, he wondered with a flicker of dread what Gretel had planned for him.

A tinny voice announced that the next stop was Glenselkie.

When they got off the train, Jack was nearly swept off his feet by a gust of wind. The professor sprang out of the train car. "Fantastic! Did you know they used to dunk witches here?"

"Dunk?" Jack imagined cups of tea and cookies.

"Drown them."

"Marvelous," Jack mumbled to the professor's back. "Hope Gretel doesn't have a meaner Scottish cousin."

They marched into the seaside town at a brisk pace, trying to keep warm. The sky was overcast, hinting at thunder. But Jack was impressed when he saw the beach. It stretched for miles, while the gray North Sea crashed and fizzed over the green rocks.

Eventually they came to a ruined castle perched over the

sea. To Jack it looked like it could tumble into the water at any moment.

They lined with the other tourists to go in, which didn't take long. Only a few excitable Americans had braved the weather to visit the castle. When they got to the ticket booth, the professor paid for them both to go in, then impatiently waved at Jack to follow him. They walked through the main part of the castle until they reached a dead end at the far wall. The roof had caved in long ago, and Jack could hear seagulls screeching above his head.

They slipped away from the other tourists and through a dank corridor which had a sign saying *Danger, do not enter.* The professor tutted and pushed it aside. They ducked under the sign and continued walking through the gloom. After several minutes, the noise of the chattering tourists had faded away and they could only hear the sound of their breathing. The professor came to an abrupt halt in front of a tarnished mirror. It had a rough piece of wood nailed over the top, and carved into it was an image of a drowning fisherman. Tiny fishing hooks had been stuck into the sides of the wood, and they tinkled softly in the breeze. Some were ancient and pitted with rust, but others were shiny and modern with familiar sporting logos on them.

"Hmm, there should be a secret fisherman's door right . . . about . . . here. Aha!" Triumphantly the professor pushed the mirror, and part of the wall slid to one side. They bent low and slipped inside the passageway, which was slimy with seaweed and shells that crunched underfoot. The professor took out a lighter and clicked on the flame to find their way. It struggled to push back the darkness, but it made them feel better. They started to walk.

Jack was amazed. "How did you know about the doorway?" he asked.

"Well, I did some research last night," the professor explained. "There was an old story that the Scottish lairds of this castle used to talk to the mermaids. Mermaids were thought to have the ability to see into the future, so the lairds would speak to them in secret and find out when their enemies were planning to attack the castle. But the advice always came at a high price." He shuddered.

Jack was confused. "Yes, but how did you know where the door was?"

"Ah, humph, beginner's luck," the professor muttered.

"Oh."

They carried on in silence after that. The passage started to slope downward and then widened. They continued to walk until finally they could see weak rays of light in the distance. The professor flicked his lighter closed, and they walked faster toward the light.

"Look, Jack, it's a cave!"

The passage ended in a large cave. Jack could hear the roar of the surf and knew they were deep under the castle, right on the edge of the wild North Sea.

As they walked, Jack thought he had never seen such a sad place. The cave walls were covered with the tattered remains of tapestries. Goblets made from pure gold lay abandoned on the ground, covered with seaweed and crab shells. Jack decided he didn't want to touch the gold. *Anything left to rot in this place has to be cursed,* he thought. At one side of the cave was a tall silver stand, etched with strange symbols. It held an enormous conch shell that was shaped like a trumpet.

The professor's eyes widened, and he reached out to touch it.

"Marvelous! See, it's so big it must have been brought here from the bottom of the deepest seas. I just wonder . . ." Frowning, he put his mouth to the bottom of the shell and blew hard, puffing out his cheeks.

A deep, eerie wailing filled the air, making the hairs on Jack's arms stand up. Even the seagulls stopped screaming.

The whole world seemed to go quiet. The professor looked uneasy.

"Maybe we should leave — you know, before some monster wakes up," Jack said, only half joking.

Suddenly a huge wave crashed into the cave. Seafoam swirled around their feet. The goblets were washed off the ground and out to sea. Jack was momentarily blinded by the salt that sprayed into the air, and when his vision cleared, he found himself staring into a pair of cold eyes.

Yelping, he splashed backward and crashed into the professor.

146

They fell to the ground. Then they scrambled to their feet and gasped.

The mermaids had arrived.

CHAPTER 14
THE DROWNED GODS

Taking a breath, Jack righted himself and turned to look at the mermaids. No matter how terrifying they were, he needed information. If only he could tell his knees to stop shaking. . . .

The three sea women had dragged themselves up into the mouth of the cave and huddled together. They balanced upright on their tails, which curled behind them like monstrous fans. Clustered so close to each other, they appeared to be a three-headed monster.

Their eyes were sightless and gray, their webbed hands curled into claws, and their skin was covered with dull gray scales. Barnacles clung to their bellies, which made them look like they had lain unmoving on the bottom of the sea for hundreds of years.

The professor cleared his throat and stuttered, "G-Good a-a-a-a-afternoon, l-l-ladies."

But the mermaids ignored him and spoke only to Jack.

"Why have you disturbed us from the watery depths?" they hissed as one, sounding like three out-of-tune violins.

"The white witch told us to come!" Jack blurted out. "Um, we guessed she might mean something about the cat — I mean your sister, who's staying with me, kind of, um . . ."

The mermaids screeched, "You lie! She has been lost to us for three hundred years. Pitiful human child, you will pay for hurting us with your lies!"

Gulping, Jack realized he was a bit out of his depth. He cursed Ariel for refusing to come with him — it would've been so much easier if she'd been there to prove he was telling the truth. Now the mermaids thought he was a liar. He stared at their gleaming scales and hooked claws. They were horribly real and could tear him to pieces whenever they felt like it.

"Maybe we should pull you to the floor of the ocean and watch your rotting skin peel like a gutted fish!" they hissed. Leaning forward, they dragged their bodies along the cave floor with their hands, slithering across the cave toward Jack.

"Your turn, professor!" Jack shouted and then sprinted to the passageway.

The professor had been standing with his mouth open since the mermaids had appeared — either in terror or admiration. He shook his head and took a deep breath. Jack watched in astonishment as the little man marched up to the creatures. He seemed to grow taller, more authoritative. Instead of his usual voice, he thundered, "Halt, I say!"

Amazingly, the mermaids stopped. Their heads swiveled as one toward the professor.

"We are here to negotiate a price for your ancient wisdom!" the professor bellowed.

Your what? Jack thought.

The mermaids continued to stare blankly at the professor.

In the tense silence, Jack heard the waves fizz into the mouth of the cave. He held his breath and waited, watching the light reflected from the sea dancing over the mermaids. They seemed to be thinking. Just as Jack had decided to call it a day and run, they spoke.

"Once, humans spoke those words to us. They knew the spells to bind us, but they always paid a heavier price than our knowledge was worth. What do you say to that, human scholar? What do you say to us, who pulled this castle down brick by brick into the sea, when we came to collect from a foolish human king?"

The professor laughed. "No price can be too much in exchange for knowledge. It's more precious than anything else. I've spent much of my life being laughed at because I wouldn't accept what others told me and pursued only what I knew was the truth. I've lost the respect of everyone for it. What price can be heavier than that?"

Jack felt sad for the professor. He'd never thought what

it must be like to be laughed at and called weird. It wasn't only the students, but the teachers did it too. With a pang of guilt, he knew he'd gone along with everybody else and laughed at the professor with them.

He also remembered a boy at school who everyone made fun of. Jack didn't like it, but he did nothing to stop it either. The boy's name was Kieran. There was nothing you could put your finger on, but he was different from everyone else. Jack remembered all the names the other kids had called him, and how they had laughed at him. It had made Jack uncomfortable.

The bullying had continued online. Someone had made a fake social media page for Kieran and posted cruel things to it. Jack had said nothing, just watched the boy become more and more lonely and sad. It kind of made him angry — why didn't Kieran stick up for himself? Why did Jack have to think about helping him? He wanted to help, but if he did, then the other kids might have turned on him too. He got so angry that, one evening in his room, he had 'liked' a particularly horrible comment. The next day, Jack had joined in the cruel laughter at school for the first time. Kieran had missed school the following week and then just never came back. Jack had seen him once in town, but Kieran had hurried away. To his dismay Jack had realized that, to Kieran, he was just one of the bullies.

Never again, he thought fiercely. In the cave, with the smell of seaweed and rotten wood in his nostrils, in the presence of monsters, he made a promise: *I'll never just go along with everyone else.*

The mermaids smiled for the first time, revealing the same razor-sharp teeth as Ariel.

"Wise words, human scholar. And your apprentice is wise too. Oh yes, we can hear your thoughts, brave human child!"

Jack jumped and hoped they hadn't *really* heard everything he was thinking. He never wanted to admit how cruel he'd been.

"Come closer then, humans. Tell us what you have to offer in exchange."

Jack and the professor inched toward the mermaids, until they stood only a foot away. *Or,* as Jack thought, *within clawing distance.*

He noticed that the sun was sinking toward the sea and hoped they wouldn't have to climb back through the passage after dark. Not with the mermaids at their back.

The professor began to tell the mermaids about Gretel, Ariel, and Jack's part in her rescue. When the mermaids heard that, they hissed through their teeth and gazed at Jack. Finally the story ended with their decision to visit the cave. Once again, the mermaids fell silent.

The professor surprised Jack by grabbing his shoulder and squeezing it. Jack felt better, just knowing there was another human in the cold cave.

Three pairs of gray eyes swiveled to look at Jack. As

one, the mermaids said, "We are forbidden to tell you the knowledge you need to fulfill the prophecy. When the white witch died on the gallows, she invoked an ancient and powerful magic that we cannot break. Nor can we tell what your own fate will be. But we can give you part of what you seek."

As the last word was uttered, the mermaids threw themselves backward into the sea and disappeared beneath the black waves.

"Was that it?" asked Jack in confusion. "A part of the prophecy is a *splash*?"

"Patience, Jack," the professor replied.

Sure enough, the mermaids hadn't finished. With a mighty spray of seawater, they surfaced as one and raised their hands above their heads. The middle mermaid held something that glinted green and gold. All three leaned in to touch the object and said, "Here are the tears we cried for our sister. They are kept in a bottle made from the glass of a murdered sailor's bottle of rum. We have treasured these tears for hundreds of years. They will help you free our sister and destroy the dark witch who stole her from us. Take the bottle — and use it wisely."

With these words, the mermaids threw the object at Jack. Not wanting to find out what they would do to him if he dropped it, Jack plucked it from the air and cradled it to his chest. The mermaids gave a final eerie screech and dove beneath the waves, never to surface again in Jack's lifetime.

Jack opened his hands and gazed at what he had been given. It was a tiny vial made from cloudy green glass and attached to a long gold chain that glittered in his hands. He tipped the bottle and saw it was full of liquid, but he had no idea what kind. The chain warmed in his fingers, but the glass remained icy cold.

A hand clapped him on the shoulder, and Jack jumped before he realized it was the professor.

"Well, m'boy," said the professor as he beamed, "that went rather well, didn't it? Hmmm?"

"I don't know," Jack replied, getting to his feet. "What exactly am I supposed to do with this?"

Jack held out the vial, and the professor's smile faltered. "Hmmmm," said the professor. "I'm sure it will all become clear. In time," he added, seeing Jack's thunderous expression.

"Time," Jack almost spat, "is something I'm running out of! You don't care, do you? This is just another interesting legend for you to study, something you can talk about in the safety of your office!"

The waves trickled through the empty cave, around the two humans. The professor appeared to be on the verge of tears. Neither of them knew what to say. Water began to slosh around their feet. The professor looked down.

"My," he exclaimed. "The tide's coming in! It's time we were heading back, I think." He avoided Jack's eyes.

Jack felt awful. He hadn't meant to shout at the professor, and now he wanted to apologize. The moment he'd spoken, he had wanted to take his harsh words back.

But the professor had already turned away. He was walking back toward the passageway, his shoulders bowed.

Jack sighed and slipped the gold chain attached to the vial over his head. It hung against his chest, and he tucked it underneath his shirt. As he followed the professor back through the gloomy passageway, Jack wondered exactly how a bottle full of monsters' tears was going to help him.

CHAPTER 15
JACK'S CHOICE

The train from Scotland slowly pulled into Manchester Piccadilly station. Jack and the professor alighted, weary and cold. It was nearly six p.m., and Jack had long stopped thinking. All he wanted was food and his bed. The two companions said their goodbyes, and Jack began to walk home from the station, completely forgetting to call his mom and tell her he had arrived. When Jack got home, his mom spent a good ten minutes scolding him.

"When you didn't call me, I got worried. I called and called you, but you didn't pick up. Can't be having you walking home in the dark, all alone," she said.

She told him to make sure he kept his cell phone switched on in the future. Jack nodded but forgot about it a few minutes later. He used to spend hours every evening on his phone, but now he wasn't interested. He had other things to think about. Plus, he didn't want his mom and dad to be able to contact him all the time. He might have to answer some awkward questions, and they would never believe the answers.

Later on that night, he sat in bed and tried for the hundredth time to decipher the white witch's prophecy. He repeated it over and over again in his head, sometimes saying it aloud, hoping that it might make more sense.

"Water and spirit must bring fire to the place where earth and air meet." Wrinkling his forehead in frustration, Jack finally gave a sigh and decided to try to get some sleep. He was having no luck understanding what he needed to do to fulfill the prophecy and had only managed to give himself a headache.

As he lay back into his pillow, Jack pulled the sparkling gold chain from under his pajama top and contemplated the vial of mermaids' tears. Ariel hadn't reacted when he had shown her the vial earlier. The little cat had simply sniffed at the bottle, then trotted away to her basket for a snooze. Jack had been a bit disappointed, thinking that Ariel might have recognized her sisters' vial. He rolled the ancient glass back and forth in his hand. Although he could hear the slosh of liquid, the glass was too cloudy to see anything inside.

Jack finally drifted off into sleep, lulled by the sound of Smash's and Ariel's soft snores from the floor.

When he woke again, Jack was not in his bed.

* * *

Jack opened his eyes and yelped in panic. He was standing in front of a grassy cliff in his pajamas. It was freezing cold, and a howling wind whistled around his shivering body. He could see the edge of the cliff and hear the pounding waves beneath. Gingerly he stepped away from the edge. *It sounds a long way down,* he thought. But that wasn't what that frightened him the most. Somehow Jack knew that he was back in Scotland, and the cliff was near the ruined castle where the mermaids had spoken to him and the professor. He was asleep, but he had been transported there.

Jack could dimly see two figures standing to his right. They were also on the cliff edge and stood facing each other. He could see the faint outline of their bodies against the black sky. They wore floor-length cloaks, one an emerald green and the other a dark scarlet. The cloaks swirled around the two figures' feet in the rising wind. Neither moved.

Jack began to back away, but then a voice like chiming bells and wolf song rang out. Although Jack still couldn't see her face, he knew it was the white witch who had visited him before.

"Here we are again, my sister in darkness. Ist thou not getting tired of our battles?" She turned to Jack and stage-whispered, "Come on, thou should be standing next to me. Show her that thou ist on the side of good and wilt stand against her!"

Jack stared at the woman in scarlet and saw his aunt's face in horrible detail. Fear seized him. He didn't think that he would be able to move. What if Gretel ran at them and threw them both off the cliff? Jack could still hear the pounding of the waves below, and he was frightened.

"You are right to feel such fear, boy," Gretel hissed, her cloak swirling around her. "I am the greatest sorceress the world has ever known, and I will not be destroyed by someone as pathetic as you."

She began to cackle, a sound horribly unlike the tinkling giggle she had used when Jack was visiting her house, before his nightmare had begun.

"If you join that stupid, soft excuse of a witch who I had hanged years ago, I will go ahead with my plan. You will be a new legend for all the children of your foolish generation. And, believe me, Jack when I say it — you will *suffer*."

From the darkness underneath her hood, Gretel almost sang, "But if you decide to join me, I may be generous and change my mind. You can walk away from all of this. You could go back to the way you were before you wandered into my house — just plain Jack Riddle again."

Her voice dropped to a whisper, becoming sweeter than syrup. Her cloak was suddenly blown by the wind toward Jack, as if reaching for him.

"There will be no more terror for you, no more black magic, no more monsters hiding in the shadows just waiting for you to come near. You can live a normal life again and stop walking in the darkness when everyone else stays in the light."

The woman in the emerald cloak gave a soft laugh. "Ah,

see, Jack, she is scared of thee. She realizes her mistake — she is terrified thou wilt succeed where so many have failed. Why else would she offer to let thee go if thou walkest away now?" She held out one hand. "Come — join me instead."

Silence fell as the two witches waited for Jack to make his decision. He took a deep breath and thought about Ariel. If he decided to walk away, the little cat, or mermaid, would stay as she was. She would never join her sisters in the sea.

Smash would stay a goblin and never remember his own name, or that he used to be a human boy — the cookie jar would remain his prison. Until, of course, another child was unlucky enough to be caught in Gretel's clutches. Then the whole thing would repeat over and over again, like some awful dark carousel ride that you couldn't get off.

He also remembered the promise he had made to himself in the mermaids' cave and knew what he had to do. He'd never been the bravest person in the world, but with a little help, he'd faced down the mermaids. He'd bet that most of the kids in his school would have run away screaming. But he, plain old Jack Riddle, had done it. And he could do it again.

Jack staggered toward the cliff edge, fighting the wind in his face. He reached the space between the two witches and deliberately turned his back on Gretel. He was more terrified than he had ever been in his life. At that moment, Jack chose his fate — he chose to stand with the white witch. He could almost feel the path he had chosen roll out before him — uncertain, dark, full of fear and hope.

Gretel screamed in fury as Jack moved away from her and toward her enemy. "You are a fool, Jack Riddle! See, then, what I have planned for you — see the spell I will cast! To punish your foolishness, it will be the most hideous spell seen in a hundred lifetimes!"

Gretel threw back her hood and revealed her second head. It snarled and showed pointed fangs, yellowed with age and rot. Then it breathed fire into the space between the two witches. Jack threw up his arms to shield himself. But the fire stopped and hovered between them.

As the fire floated in the air, he saw there was something in the center. Horrified, Jack let out a quiet moan.

It was a statue. It looked exactly like Jack. But he gazed into the statue's terrified eyes and knew that it wasn't just a statue — it actually *was* him.

Gretel was going to turn him into stone. But he would still be alive — unable to move, or let anyone know that his mind and soul were still there, trapped inside a stone prison. The statue stood in the middle of a garden, in what looked like a deserted park. There was no one in sight except a stray dog, thin to the point of starvation, wandering a few feet from the statue's base. It felt like a sad place.

The ball of fire faded, and Jack could see Gretel once more. She and her second head were grinning at him. He didn't know when he had begun to cry, but tears were running down his face.

"I really am ever so pleased with myself, Jackie-Poo. You'll make such a lovely ornament!"

"But why?" Jack whispered.

Gretel faltered for a second. "Why? Because your generation is obsessed with those ridiculous gadgets you call cell phones! You laze around all day like stupid stone statues, ignoring everyone and everything around you. And all I can hear is the tap-tap-tapping of screens and the occasional irritating beeping noises." She leaned in and said confidentially, "In all my long years, I truly have never seen a more self-absorbed and idle generation of children! So let's see how you like being a REAL living statue — for all eternity!"

With a triumphant laugh, Gretel jumped over the cliff. Jack gasped and ran to the edge, hoping for a wonderful moment that she had fallen onto the rocks below. But then a hideous bat, the size of a horse, flew into the air carrying Gretel on its back. With a cheery wave, she kicked the bat's sides and flew away over the sea, her cloak rippling in the wind.

Jack covered his face with his hands. This spell was far worse than he'd ever thought it would be. He then felt a cool hand on his shoulder, and he turned to face the white witch.

"Oh dear," she sighed. "Always so dramatic. She cannot simply disappear in a puff of smoke like every other self-respecting wicked witch." Then she smiled, her teeth gleaming white against her black lipstick. "And well done, Jack. I was impressed with thee for standing up to her. Who knows? Perhaps thou really dost have a chance at finally understanding how to defeat Gretel."

She rolled her neck, and the bones cracked. "Just as well, really. I am so ready to retire from this game. Shall we call it a night? Oh, but I must give thee a second hint before I go!"

Feeling shaken, but quite proud of the way he'd stood up to Gretel, Jack gave a tentative smile. He opened his mouth to say thank you, but the cliff seemed to be dissolving in front of his eyes. The white witch was also changing, becoming more transparent.

"Listen carefully, Jack." Her voice was quieter this time, fading along with the landscape. "Thou must go and visit the wild fairy folk. But be warned — they are tricky and dangerous creatures. The fairy folk will do anything to get their magic back from Gretel, but they will never be on thy side, and they will harm thee if they can."

She was almost gone now. Jack could clearly see his bedroom. He was standing next to his bed, and the cliffs were like a hazy impression left over from a vivid dream.

Finally, he could only see the outline of the white witch's hood. She whispered, "Remember: they care nothing for humans except as a way to entertain themselves. They like to watch humans suffer."

Jack blinked and suddenly he was back in his bed. Ariel jumped up and gently patted his pajama top with one paw. He stroked her fluffy head. Purring, Ariel cuddled in, and they drifted off into a blessedly dreamless sleep.

CHAPTER 16

OUT OF TIME

The alarm woke Jack the next morning. He leaped upright, gasping, and held his hands out. For a moment there, he had been convinced they were made of stone. Relieved to see that his hands were normal, just shaking a little, he pushed Ariel to the floor, got up, and went to the bathroom to get dressed. Smash wasn't in his basket; Jack assumed that he was downstairs.

Jack walked into the kitchen with Ariel trotting at his heels. Smash was sitting in a toddler's high chair guzzling a bowl of milk mixed with honey, sugar, and whipped cream.

"He'll get ruddy fat if you keep feeding him so much sugar," Mr. Riddle warned Mrs. Riddle, who just smiled sappily at Smash. When they noticed Jack hovering in the doorway, Mr. Riddle bellowed, "You, my lad, have some explaining t'do!"

Jack just stared blankly at him, trying to think what his

dad was talking about. It could have been any number of things, with all that had been happening lately.

His father waved a letter. "This Mr. Scrimp says that you've been bringing illegal animals into school!"

Jack's heart fell. *Mr. Scrimp must be out of the hospital and well again,* he thought. He probably wasn't too happy with Jack either, considering he had accidentally set Smash on him. And embarrassed him in front of the school. And put him in the hospital . . .

"Well, don't you have anything to say? You feel like telling me why you're throwing away your education by messing around when you should be studying? Do you know that I have never *once* heard someone say 'I'm so happy that I didn't work hard when I was at school. Failing all my exams really improved my life!' And what about this all-day history trip you went on the other day? Do you really think that spending all your time studying history will help you with your core subjects, like math and science? What job can you get doing history? Next time tell your history teacher that you need to stay in school and not go gallivanting off doing fluffy subjects for the day!" Mr. Riddle turned redder as he lectured his son. "You just don't understand how important it is to pass your core exams. And I'll tell you another thing. . . ."

Jack felt fury building up inside him. It was bad enough he had the world's — no, history's — most evil witch after him. He couldn't even tell his parents about it, because they would never believe him!

"Why d'you care?" Jack shouted. "You never talk to me anymore — you just sit there and look miserable. And you shout all the time. You hate me, and guess what — I hate you too!" Grabbing his bag, Jack stormed from the kitchen.

Mr. Riddle gasped. "How *dare* you walk away from me! Come back here right this minute!"

Biting his lip so it wouldn't wobble, Jack didn't turn around. Stopping only to give Smash a pat on the head, he strode out of the kitchen and onto the street, Ariel at his heels.

He told himself that the wetness he felt on his cheeks was from the morning drizzle.

* * *

The professor met Jack at the school gates, looking gritty-eyed, as though he hadn't slept in some time.

"Jack, m'boy, you look awfully chipper this morning, I must say! Lots of color in your cheeks. Morning, Miss Ariel. Remember that you must put her in your bag, Jack. The school is awfully jumpy about animals on the premises ever since the, uh, unfortunate incident with Mr. Scrimp."

Jack blurted out, "I had another dream! You know, with the white witch. But this time Gretel was there, and she told me she was going to turn me into a living statue!"

"Oh," replied the professor, blinking. He pushed one hand through his hair. "That sounds abominable. Bad enough to be turned to stone, but to be kept alive inside a stone prison, unable to move or speak for eternity . . . Did she say anything else?"

"Well, she did get quite annoyed when I said I wouldn't join the forces of darkness, but —"

"No, no, I mean what did the white witch say?"

Irritated that the professor didn't seem at all bothered about the fact that he had spent his night standing up to an evil witch, Jack huffed and started to walk through the gates. Ariel meowed and raced after him, twining around his ankles.

"Go home!" Jack snapped. "Why can't you act like a normal cat and, I dunno, spend your days chasing mice or something? You're drawing way too much attention to me. Go on, get! You can't come to school unless you'll stay hidden in my bag. And look what happened last time I tried that!"

But the cat just sniffed and stayed close to his feet.

The professor jogged to keep up. "Come on, Jack, don't be like that. Tell me what she said! She's a good witch — she must have told you something we can use?"

Jack slowed down. He sighed and reached down to grab Ariel. "Fine," he said to the animal. "You can come with me. But you're staying in the bag." He dropped her into his bag and, to his surprise, she didn't instantly try to claw and bite her way out of it. He patted her gently on the head before closing the bag. Turning back to the professor, he said, "Well, she did tell me to go and visit the fairies. They don't sound very nice, though. Bit sketchy, actually."

By this time, the other students were all arriving. They wandered past, their collars turned up against the cold, yawning and blinking. Jack carried on describing his dream.

The professor listened intently, murmuring under his breath when he heard more about the white witch's command to see the fairies.

Then the professor grabbed Jack's arm and dragged him through the main doors. "We must go on another emergency field trip!" he said, pulling a bunch of forms from his pocket. They fluttered to the ground, and he tutted, bending to scoop them up.

"What, again?" Jack wailed. He folded his arms and refused to budge. "What about school? Don't get me wrong, I'd normally want to get out of it, but my dad keeps yelling at me about missing important classes and —"

To Jack's surprise, the professor started to shout.

"Yes, again! Gretel is accelerating. The white witch was right to come and warn you. We must move fast, because the next time you see Gretel, she will cast her living statue spell on you." He shuddered and lowered his voice. "I'm afraid that we've run out of time. We can no longer worry about normal things like missing school. Your life is in very great danger. We must go tomorrow morning at the very earliest, or I fear the worst."

Jack was about to protest that he didn't care. That no matter what he did, everyone around him seemed to be angry with him these days. But then he snapped his mouth shut. An icy tingle of fear spread through his stomach. Something awful was going to happen to him if they didn't figure out how to fulfill the prophecy. And he thought that the witch probably had worse punishments up her sleeve than his parents did.

"OK," he sighed, beaten. "Let's go."

"Excellent." The professor beamed. "Make sure to bring Ariel this time. Oh, and the goblin too — they could be useful. And don't worry too much about the fairies. They generally only kill you if they're bored."

CHAPTER 17
THE ELEMENTS

Where earth and air meet. Where earth and air meet. The phrase kept repeating itself in Jack's head. The train he was on chugged away, sounding like it was also repeating the prophecy. But what did it mean? Jack felt haunted by the words.

They were on their way to Stonehenge. The professor said Stonehenge had a doorway to the dark fairy world. He was convinced that the ancient stone circle was the only way to find the fairies — who, after all, weren't exactly going to be hanging around Jack's estate, just waiting to be found.

Jack had been worried about what his parents would say about another history trip, but his dad was oddly subdued when Jack got in from school. His mom had looked at the permission slip, then said loudly, "Of course you should go. This teacher says you're his best student. That's a great achievement, Jack."

Mr. Riddle had glowered at the TV set but said nothing.

Mrs. Riddle had ignored her husband and said, "Just remember to give me a call when you get to the station this time so I can pick you up. Do you need me to drop you off in the morning?"

"Uh, no," Jack had said. He was confused by the feeling of tension in the room. "I have to go into school first to get the principal to sign the form."

At school Jack had handed the slip to Mr. Scrimp, who'd narrowed his eyes at Jack but couldn't think of a reason to refuse. The principal had temporarily lost his voice in shock, because of his encounter with Smash. Now out of the hospital and with no voice, Mr. Scrimp used flashcards to give orders to teachers. Most of them simply turned their back on him and pretended not to see him, which did not improve Mr. Scrimp's mood. To Jack, the principal had scribbled *Fine — but I'm watching you, Riddle* on a flashcard and raised his eyebrows menacingly. So Jack was able to go on the trip to Stonehenge, although he would have much preferred a week of detention.

As they had left the school, Jack had walked past Hannah, Ayo, and Liam, who were going to their next class. Jack stopped to talk to them, and the professor strode ahead, oblivious to the fact that he had lost his student.

"Where're you going?" Hannah asked, her bag swinging. As Jack had predicted, she smacked a younger boy on the head, and he fell to the ground in pain.

"Whoops!" she said. "You should watch where you're going."

"Um, I have to do community service," Jack explained. "You know, Scrimp thinks I let that animal loose in the school. So my punishment is to be pulled out of school to do some boring helpful stuff."

"Ah." They nodded wisely.

"In a retirement home cleaning the toilets!" Jack said wildly. Inwardly, he groaned, wondering what on earth made him say that.

"Eww, gross!" they all cried.

At that moment the professor had realized his charge was missing.

"Jack!" he bellowed from outside the school gates. "Keep up, lad!"

Ayo, Hannah, and Liam had shuffled off, giving Jack sympathetic looks.

Now Jack was seated on a train with the professor, Ariel, and Smash. The professor had said they should bring the two creatures along, just in case they needed some more help. He was taking no chances with the fairies, he said. Jack just prayed that the cat and goblin wouldn't somehow wreak destruction on the train after he had managed to smuggle them on board.

Smash sat happily next to Jack, eating the contents of the candy cart that the professor had kindly bought from the conductor. Pieces of plastic wrapper kept flying into the air and hitting other passengers in the head as Smash munched.

Luckily people just glared at Jack and the professor, with a few muttering loudly about how they should control their pet monkey better.

Ariel had curled up in the seat next to the window. She was mesmerized by the view.

The professor had a large leather-bound book perched on his knee, and he murmured the words aloud as he read. Jack watched him, wondering when he was going to find out what would happen at Stonehenge.

The professor happened to look up from his book. Catching Jack's eye, he smiled. "Just doing some extra research on the prophecy. The more I look at it, the more I think you're right — the fairies might be able to help us. But the white witch was correct; they are dangerous creatures. They're far more dangerous than the mermaids, and we only just managed to persuade *them* to help us."

Jack automatically put his hand on the vial of tears that the mermaids had given him, which still hung around his neck. It comforted him slightly to know it was there.

Frowning and pinching the bridge of his nose in concentration, the professor pulled out the piece of parchment with the prophecy on it and recited, "*First comes the goblin, then the witch. Destruction will rain down on thy children's heads. It will always be thus for several hundred years, unless water and spirit bring fire to the place where earth and air meet.*"

Jack said, "Well, I still don't know what she was rambling on about, no matter how many times we repeat it. Don't you think it would've helped if she just told me last night what she meant?"

Laughing, the professor said, "But then it wouldn't be a quest, would it? There are rules, Jack — all magic must have rules."

The professor continued to stare into space. His forehead began to lose its frown, and his eyes suddenly lit up with excitement.

"Jack," he asked, "what if it's talking about the elements? You know, earth, air, fire, and water?"

"The what?"

"The elements form our world. Our ancestors stole that knowledge from the fairies. Bit of a mistake. The fairies were most displeased." The professor's face darkened for a moment. "Anyway, it can't just be any old water or fire. They must be magical objects. But what are they? And how do we use them?"

Jack bit his lip and thought of something. "We already have some water, Professor, remember? The mermaids gave it to us."

The professor froze for a moment, then lifted his head to stare at Jack. "By jove," he whispered, "you're right! We've had part of the answer all this time, and I didn't realize! You are a clever one. We just need to get the next clue from the fairies at Stonehenge."

Jack grabbed a packet of chips from Smash. The goblin growled, then dug into the pile of food next to him to find another one.

Ripping open the bag and taking a handful of salty chips, Jack nodded. "Yeah, I wanted to ask about that. Why Stonehenge? I'm surprised you didn't give me a long lecture before we boarded the train."

From her seat next to the window, Ariel gave a little chuckle.

Raising his eyebrows, the professor said indignantly, "I do not give long lectures! Or, at least, when I do, they are interesting." He paused. "Well, anyway. Do you want to find out or not?"

Jack grinned. "Sure."

Clearing his throat, the professor continued. "Stonehenge is a mystery. It's a ring of stones that are perfectly lined up with the stars. No one knows why it was built. And no normal men could've carried the stones to the hillside, or understood how to line them up so they exactly mirror the stars in the sky."

He tapped the book on his lap. "According to this banned book, which I, uh, borrowed from the private library of the British Museum, there is a radical theory that it must have been one of the great ancient races that built it." The professor paused and then leaned forward. "It was either the giants or the fairies."

Jack sat back in his seat to listen. He plucked Ariel from her space by the window and settled her on his lap. Lazily, she stretched, then settled down to snooze again. Even Smash stopped chewing quite so loudly. They were all soothed by the sound of the professor's voice and the story of vicious giants walking the earth.

"The giants were born when the mountains became lonely," the professor continued, reading aloud from the book in his hand. "The mountains could not speak to each other, and they were tired of listening to the wind. So they created the giants. They were fifty feet tall at least and thickly muscled. They had teeth like elephant tusks, and brains the size of a squirrel. This meant they were strong — but very stupid. They eventually killed each other after wars that lasted many hundreds of years. The unfortunate thing about giants was that they loved to hold grudges and had no sense of reason — they would insult each other, fight, then make up. *Then* they'd forget they'd made up and fight all over again. So they fought and fought until they all died, in long, bloody battles."

The train juddered to a halt. More people got on. The professor stopped speaking and closed the book carefully, so no one could see its contents.

Jack sighed. The professor was paranoid about being seen as insane, he realized. But Jack wanted to hear more. He had no idea that giants had roamed the earth. He knew about dinosaurs — giant lizards — he had studied them in school and had been to see their fossilized remains in a museum. So he supposed it made sense that there were once giant humans too.

More people came into the train car. Finally, when

everyone was seated, the conductor blew his whistle, and the train rattled into action once more.

The professor cleared his throat and lifted the book to begin reading again. "So," he said, "where was I? Ah yes, the giants killed each other after several long and bloody wars. But what page was I on? Hmm."

Smash grinned and wiggled forward in his seat. Absently, the professor smiled at the little goblin, trying to find his place in the book again.

A tingle ran down Jack's spine. Looking back, he would never be able to say why, but he suddenly felt as though they were in danger. Gazing around the car, he couldn't see any reason for his unease. Still wary, he turned back to the professor.

"Yes, yes, here we are, the legend of the giants, part two. When the giants were on the verge of being wiped out, the mountains grieved. They would miss their children but knew that they couldn't just create more giants because they would all murder each other again. So the mountains instructed the last living giants to carve pieces of stone from the tips of the mountaintops. The giants carried these massive stones to the plain in Salisbury and placed them where the mountains had told them. They called it Stonehenge."

The professor paused and raised a bushy white eyebrow at Ariel.

"And the stones were exactly aligned with the stars in the sky. The stones were a gateway for eerie creatures who lived in the bowels of the earth to pass through. These creatures had been imprisoned there millions of years before by the stars in punishment for their cruelty. They were called the fairy folk. The mountains adopted them as their new children, hoping they would be more peaceful than the giants. But they could only watch in sorrow as the fairies lived wicked lives."

Jack's spine began to tingle again. He felt dizzy and watched as a shadow fell over the professor's book.

"Tickets, please," a sweet voice said.

The professor closed his book and, without looking up, rummaged in his pockets for the tickets. "Why, of course. If I can just remember where I put them. . . ." He frowned and patted his coat. "Hmm. I could have sworn they were in my coat pocket — nope, they must be in my bag. . . ."

Jack looked up and wanted to scream, but he was struck dumb with horror. Standing over them, wearing a conductor's uniform, was Gretel.

She wore a blond wig and horn-rimmed glasses to hide her eyes, but Jack knew it was her. He could never forget that voice. The conductor's hat covered up her other revolting head. It seemed to move slightly, although no one would notice because of the swaying of the train.

Leaping up in her seat, Ariel hissed and spat. Smash gagged on the packet of chips he had just poured into his mouth, spraying crumbs all over the professor.

"Honestly, Smash, what have we talked about? If you

can't eat chips quietly, then you can only have chocolate!" the professor said sternly.

He kept patting his pockets, a faint look of panic on his face. "Oh dear, I'm sure they were in this pocket! Aha!" he said triumphantly. "Found them!"

All Jack could think was, *He doesn't realize it's her! What can I do? What can I do?*

In a daze, Jack watched as the professor handed their tickets to Gretel. She held them up and shook her head. "Tut, tut, it looks as if someone has given you the wrong tickets! You'll have to all come with me, I'm afraid."

"Really?" said the professor. "How extraordinary. I could've sworn they were the right ones. Jack," he said, turning toward him, "did you notice anything unusual about the tickets? I say, you look rather pale, young chap. You feeling all right?"

Jack couldn't speak. His voice seemed to be locked inside his throat, held there by fear. All he could think about was his dream from the other night. The image of Gretel flying away on a giant bat and screeching that he had chosen his fate and would be turned to stone. Now, in the harsh light of the train, she smiled at him and began to slip her hand into her pocket. Jack realized with horror that she was reaching for her wand.

Beads of sweat broke out on Jack's forehead. The rest of the train car seemed to fade away. All his attention was focused on Gretel's triumphant face as her hand tightened on the wand in her pocket.

Then a ball of white fur flew past his face, breaking his trance. Ariel, seeing what was about to happen, had launched herself into the air. Hissing, she sprang onto Gretel's face and landed claws first. She sank them into Gretel's face and hung on, drawing blood.

Gretel shrieked and grabbed Ariel, trying to pull her off. The professor's mouth fell open. "Ariel! What in God's name . . ."

Jack's tongue unfroze and he gasped, "It's Gretel! Run!"

The professor's eyes widened, and he gaped in horror. "Gretel? But —"

Jack leaped to his feet. "Get up, we have to get out of here! She's got her wand!"

CHAPTER 18
GRETEL'S REVENGE

Smash jumped down from his seat to the floor. Reaching up, he grabbed the professor's hand and pulled him though the train car. Jack tried to follow, but his path was instantly blocked by a stampede of passengers all rushing to help the conductor.

Gretel was screaming and lying on the floor, still trying to pull Ariel from her face. Some of the passengers were attempting to dislodge the cat without taking out Gretel's eye. But, with a horrible popping sound, Ariel suddenly let go — triumphantly taking a trailing, bloody eyeball with her!

The cat dropped it and scuttled underneath the seats. Gretel's eyeball lay in a soggy pile on the floor.

"Dear lord!" shouted a man in a pinstriped suit, hovering behind the crowd.

Gretel flung back her head and let out an unearthly, rage-filled shriek, throwing her hands to her face.

"We must get you to the hospital at once!" cried a matronly looking woman. She pulled out her cell phone, fingers poised to dial 911.

"Out of my way, mortal scum!" Gretel hissed, brandishing her wand. The professor and all the passengers froze, then gracefully slithered to the ground, sound asleep. They started to snore gently. Smash dove behind the candy cart, sending candy and chips showering to the floor.

Gretel dragged herself along the ground toward the seat where Ariel was hiding. She reached out one hand and started to grope underneath it. "Come to Gretel, little fishy! Come here so I can THROTTLE YOU!"

Panicking, Jack tried to find a way to lead her away from the cat. But he was trapped in a corner. Gretel blocked the aisle, and the other way was littered with sleeping bodies. Jack looked around wildly and saw the window behind him. With a gulp, he decided to take drastic action.

He stood on a seat and unlocked the window, feeling the wind blasting through the open window. Turning his head, he shouted, "Hey Gretel! It's me! Come and get me if you can!"

Gretel flicked her head around and growled. She began to crawl toward the window like a deadly spider.

"Uh, oh," Jack muttered. He gingerly lifted one foot, then the other, through the window to rest on a tiny ledge outside. He wriggled the rest of his body through and gripped the window frame for dear life. Then one foot suddenly slipped.

The ground whooshed away in a dizzying blur of colors as he struggled to keep his grip.

"*WhatamIdoing?* This is crazy!" he screamed into the wind.

He pulled his foot back up, turned his body to face the train, and managed to keep both feet balanced on the thin ledge. Gasping in panic, Jack gripped the window frame with slippery fingers and clung on.

Then Gretel's face loomed in front of him. She was staggering toward the window, her wand raised.

Jack moaned. He had no other option. He had to climb onto the roof of the train! Trembling uncontrollably, he let go of the window frame and gripped the top of the train above his head with one hand, then the other.

"They make it look so easy in the movies!" he whimpered.

Feeling as though his arms were about to be ripped from their sockets, he somehow managed to drag up his right foot and hook it over the edge of the roof above him. Heart hammering, he jumped with all his strength. His arms screaming in pain, he pulled his body up over his hands and rolled onto the roof.

"*Yes!*" he gasped. "I did it, I did it, I DID IT! And I'm not dead!"

Jack dragged himself farther up and away from the edge. The wind roared over his head. He couldn't stand up. He knew that if he didn't lie flat, he would be pitched like a leaf off the side of the train and onto the tracks.

Lying there, exhausted, he hoped his friends had been able to hide somewhere on the train.

A clattering sound broke into his thoughts. He lifted his head. A hand had appeared on the edge of the roof — a dainty hand covered with blood. Gretel was trying to pull herself up.

"No way!" Jack wailed.

Swallowing hard, he crawled back toward the edge. The wind screamed in his ears as he moved. He had to push Gretel's hand off and knock her from the train! He shrank from the thought of it. He had no idea if he'd actually be able to grab that horrible hand. And even if she was trying to cast a hideous spell on him, he wasn't sure he could hurt someone else that badly. But he knew he had no choice. He had to try to save himself.

Before he even got close, a flash of light cracked in the sky. The clouds turned a deep purple and rain began to sheet to the ground. Jack started to slide toward the edge of the train as the water made him lose his grip. Wailing and trying desperately not to fall off, Jack dug his fingers into the grooves between the metal and clung on. Then he turned his head and saw with despair that Gretel had pulled herself onto the roof and now stood a few feet away from him. She balanced perfectly on the train like a ballerina as the rain streamed down. Thunder rolled overhead. Jack knew he was cornered.

Gretel's face was covered in blood, and it streamed down toward her chin. An empty hole gaped where her right eye had been. She lifted her wand and pointed it toward the sky.

"Enough games. As much fun as hunting you has been, what with the opening of the cookie jar and our little trips through the dream realms and all, it's time to show my real power. Like my little storm, Jackie-poo?" she asked sarcastically. Jack winced. He really didn't want to be remembered as "Jackie-poo."

Gretel grinned, her empty eye socket dark and somehow alive. The wind whipped the conductor's hat from her head, and her second face glared down at Jack. Its shriveled skin repelled the rain. It remained dry and cracked despite the downpour, which soaked Jack to the bone.

Jack lay at her feet and waited for the wand to be pointed at him. He waited for the flash of light that would stop his breath and leave him trapped in a stone prison for eternity.

"You know, Jackie-poo," Gretel said, tapping her chin with her wand, "I was *so* disappointed the other night when you took *her* side instead of mine." Lightning ripped through the clouds again, illuminating Gretel's face. She took a step forward and stood on Jack's hand. The bones in his hand ground together, and he closed his eyes, groaning in pain.

Gretel carried on, as if she hadn't noticed. "It would have been so nice if someone, for once — JUST ONCE — took my side in these matters."

Thoughtfully, she lowered her wand and pointed it

at Jack's head. "But I really don't think anybody will ever understand the important work I do. Just think of the children whose manners I improve by showing them what happens to naughty, disobedient brats like you, Jackie-poo." She paused and slowly lowered her wand. As she spoke, Jack felt the last of his hope shrivel up and die.

Gretel laughed. "Don't think there's anyone brave enough to stop me. It's just you and me, Jackie, and it's time to cast my spell. You want to laze around all day on your phone, hmmm? I'll make it so you never have to move again. You can sit still for the rest of your life. I'm going to turn you into a living statue as a warning to all those self-obsessed brats who just can't stop TAPPETY-TAP-TAPPING!"

With an almighty effort, Jack looked up at her. Even though it meant he had to look at someone evil, he still wanted to see something, anything, one more time before he was turned to stone. She was ranting, her hands raised over her head. Rain lashed down around her.

"This will send a message to every spoiled, lazy child out there with one of those fiendish instruments: a chattering, ringing, noisy, loathsome cell phone!" In a rage she raised her wand and pointed it at Jack.

But the crack of blinding white light didn't appear. Instead, a can of soda sailed through the air — and smashed into Gretel's raw, empty eye socket.

Gretel screamed. Her hand flew to her face. She was thrown off balance as she covered her eye in pain. With a scream of fury, she fell from the roof into the rushing darkness below. She was gone.

Jack whipped his head round to see Smash standing on the other side of the train roof. The goblin had a slingshot in his hands made from empty packets of chips and gummy bears. Smash galloped across the metal roof and skidded to a halt beside Jack.

"Smaaasssshhh taaakkke dooown!" he chortled.

With that, Jack promptly passed out.

CHAPTER 19
STONEHENGE

When Jack woke, he could feel the gentle rhythm of the train. He opened his eyes and saw the professor's anxious face looming over him. With a groan, Jack sat up and asked, "What happened this time?"

Sighing with relief, the professor replied, "You fainted, dear boy. Smash had to drag you back into the train. You do seem to faint quite a lot — maybe you ought to have your blood pressure checked?"

Jack snorted. "Or maybe I'm just not used to being chased across train roofs by a wicked witch, then being rescued by a goblin with a slingshot and sugar issues?"

From underneath the seat, Smash giggled.

The professor ignored them both and carried on, "Well, we seem to have lost Gretel for the time being. I wish I could say that's the last we'll hear from her, but she doesn't die that easily. She's wounded, though, so we should have enough time to visit the stone circle before she finds us again."

Jack shivered at the thought of the stone circle. The gateway to the fairy kingdom. He remembered the pictures from the professor's book, which showed an evil-looking creature with a bow and arrow made from wooden splinters and strung with spiderwebs.

He stared around the train and smiled faintly. The other passengers were all still snoring away.

Gretel was nowhere to be seen.

"How did you wake up?" Jack asked.

The professor raised one eyebrow and looked at Ariel, who was calmly sitting back in her original seat and washing her paws. "Ariel jumped up and down on my ribs until I woke up. Surprisingly effective. And painful!" He shot the cat a dark look.

At that moment the train lurched to a stop, tossing Ariel to the floor with an unladylike thump. She hissed, then jumped onto Jack's shoulder. They had arrived at Stonehenge.

The other passengers stirred. Embarrassed mutters of "Oh, pardon me," and "What am I doing on the floor?" could be heard as people scrambled to their feet.

The professor stood up and shoved his books into a backpack. Smash scurried out from under the seats and sat at Jack's feet.

"Come on, Jack, let's go and see if the legends about

the fairy folk are true." The professor strode down the aisle, picking his way through the confused passengers.

Jack stuffed Smash head-first into the bag and picked it up, saying to the grumbling goblin, "Cheer up, at least you won't be walking." He followed the professor to the train platform.

* * *

Twenty minutes later, the professor was arguing with the ticket taker at the entrance to Stonehenge. "But we must go into the ruins, sir, it's a matter of academic necessity!"

The ticket taker sighed. He had heard it all before. Stonehenge had been closed to the public several years ago and a big fence built around the stones. Since then, hundreds of tourists had tried to threaten or bribe him into letting them walk around the stones. He gloomily thought that he would have been able to retire if he had a dollar for each tourist who had tried to get past him.

"Y'see, Professor . . . uh, what was it again?" the ticket taker said, running his hands through his hair. "Oh yes, Professor Footnote — we can't let anyone in. Them stones, y'see, they've been eroding from all the tourists trampling around. If we carried on letting people walk willy-nilly around them, why, there'd be none left in another hundred or so years. You'll just have to stand in front of the fence and look in, like everyone else does." The inspector smiled and then barked, "Next!"

The couple behind them pushed in front and began to ask

the exact same questions. The ticket taker reached for his cup of coffee under the counter and took a massive slurp.

Jack and the professor walked around the back of the ticket booth. "Think, Ambrosius, think," the professor growled. It took Jack a minute to remember that it was the professor's first name. "How can we get to those blasted stones?"

"Well, couldn't we just pretend we didn't realize you aren't allowed in and, um, climb the fence?" Jack asked.

Ariel glared up at him with scorn.

"Maybe it is a bit high to climb. . . ." Jack muttered.

They joined another group of tourists who were making their way up the hill. A self-important guide was droning on about the history of the site and all the different theories about where it came from.

"Of course," the guide said, "we realize that the stones were most likely carved by Neolithic man, who used them as a graveyard. Hundreds of bodies have been found buried under the central altar."

The group walked faster, hoping to see something grisly through the barbed wire fence around the stones.

A little boy with a pout tugged his mother's hand and shrieked, "Mommy, I want to go in and see the bones! Mommy!"

The boy's mother started to ask the tour guide why they couldn't go in. Jack felt a pang of sympathy for him. *If I worked here,* Jack thought, *I'd be tempted to have the reason tattooed on my forehead, just to stop the constant questions.*

They got to the top of the hill. The wind whipped around them. Jack felt the hairs on the back of his neck go up. It was a strange place. Most of the stones had fallen down, but you could see where they must have stood. The remaining upright stones were at least twelve feet high. They were arranged in a circle around a massive altar.

The professor whispered, "There's a gateway inside that stone altar — a door to the fairy world."

The little boy, who was covered in snot from crying, shrieked, "Mommy, that man said there're fairies in there! I wanna see the fairies — now!"

The rest of the group turned and glared at the professor, who smiled weakly. A woman with a mouth like a chewed lemon whispered, "He's a crazy old man."

The little boy giggled. Ariel promptly hissed at him and the boy yelped, then hid behind his mother's legs.

Ariel jumped elegantly to the ground, squeezed under the fence, and trotted to the center of the stone circle. She leaped onto the altar and sat there, watching Jack and the professor. None of the other tourists noticed. They were too busy fighting over the best place to take selfies.

Jack gasped. *Of course*, he thought. *We could dig under the fence*! He whispered his idea to the professor, who smiled and said, "Great idea, but how do we distract the rest of the group?"

People had started to wander off around the edges of the fence, peering through at the ruins. Many of them seemed a bit bored at this point, because after all, Stonehenge was just a bunch of broken stones. But they would still notice if Jack and the professor crawled underneath the fence.

Smash began to wriggle inside Jack's backpack. Jack turned to the professor. They both shrugged, as if to say, why not? Jack opened the bag and dumped Smash on the ground. Smash stretched and reached his tiny hands up to move the rusty bells on his jester's cap. They jingled softly. The little boy, who was still hovering next to them, heard the bells.

He immediately came out from behind his mother's legs and toddled toward Smash. Jack suddenly understood — they needed a diversion, and Smash was going to give them one.

Jack tapped the professor on the arm and pointed. The professor looked confused, then saw the little boy and Smash standing together. They were almost nose to nose. Understanding dawned across the professor's face.

The little boy reached down to grab Smash's hat. "Mommy, I want that hat! I want, want, want the hat! Give it to me, nasty monkey!"

Smash grinned, showing his sharp teeth, and let the little boy pull off his hat. Then he growled. The little boy froze and yelped, "No, hat mine. Bad monkey!"

The little boy started to run down the hill. Smash chased him, still growling.

The boy's mother turned around and squealed, "Stay away from my precious Frederick, you horrible creature!"

Then the whole group turned to see the little boy running down the hill, with Smash chasing him and the mother chasing Smash. The tour guide mumbled something about being sued and yelped, "Come on everyone, help me catch the monkey!"

Nobody moved.

"Fine," he sighed. "Free pastries for the first person to help me catch it!"

A stampede of tourists pushed each other out of the way to run after Smash, with the tour guide running after them.

The professor walked swiftly to the fence and started digging with his hands. Jack joined him, pulling away clumps of dank dirt from the ground. In a matter of minutes, the wet soil had been pulled away, and the professor squeezed under the fence.

"Come on, Jack," puffed the professor. "We don't have much time before they get back and realize we're gone!"

Jack hesitated. He felt as if there was a giant spotlight on his back. Surely someone would notice them? He risked a quick glance over his shoulder. No one was watching them. They were all still too busy running after Smash, who was merrily zigzagging down the hill.

Jack ducked under the fence, feeling the loose dirt trickle down his neck.

They pulled themselves free and raced to the stone altar where Ariel was sitting and scrambled up next to her.

"Uh," said Jack, "now what?"

The professor pulled off his backpack and reached in for the book he had been reading on the train.

"Now, m'boy, we open the gateway."

"I get that, but how?"

"We chant the fairy rhyme stating that we come here of our own free will and accept any ghastly consequences."

Jack nearly jumped off the stone altar. "Sounds lovely," he said with a scowl.

The professor grinned and opened the book. Jack could see that the page was covered in strange symbols and had a skull drawn above the words of the spell.

"Hear me, ancient guardians of the stones," the professor cried. The pages of the book ruffled in a sudden gust of icy wind, flying back from his hands. "Blasted wind. So where was I? Ah yes. The summoning spell on page 666." He cleared his throat and continued. "Hear me, ancient guardians of the stones, I request your power to open the door to the fairy kingdom. Though my flesh may blacken and shrivel and my eyes be replaced by toads, I still demand my rite of passage to the darkest bowels of the Earth. Grant me this boon, oh guardians, and I accept all that may befall me."

Fantastic, Jack thought, *that's just what we need — more ghastly consequences.*

The wind seemed to die down. All was still. Ariel began to hiss. She didn't like the power that had started to gather around them. It hummed in the air and made them shiver. But nothing else happened.

Jack smiled and said with relief, "Oh well, never mind, better luck next time. I saw an ice cream truck on the way up. How about we just go back and —"

Then the stones began to sing.

CHAPTER 20
FAIRY FIRE

The stones were humming a high-pitched, awful song. It sounded like a zombie's nails being dragged up and down a gravestone. Jack and the professor clamped their hands over their ears, but they couldn't shut it out.

"Hold on to the altar, Jack!" the professor cried. "You must hold on, no matter what happens next!"

"What d'you mean? What's going to happen?"

The altar began to rock and groan, the massive hinges creaking as it tipped straight up into the air.

"Aaaaarrrrrgggggghhhhh!" Jack cried.

The three of them fell into the gap beneath the stone, which slammed back into place behind them.

Shrieking, they slid down a dark passageway deep underground. Flaming torches lit the edges of the tunnel. Statues of repulsive gargoyles stood between the torches.

197

They leered at the trespassers as they fell down and down into the inky blackness.

Finally they landed with a crash at the bottom of the tunnel.

Jack found his feet first. Gasping, he helped the professor stand up. Ariel was spitting in anger.

"Shut up, Ariel," Jack whispered. "We don't know what's down here."

The professor got to his feet and instantly bent over, coughing. "I'm far too old for this," he croaked.

When the professor had recovered, they looked around to see where they were. They were standing in a long corridor, which was also lined with torches and statues. But these weren't gargoyles. These appeared to be wax dummies and were of warriors from all different parts of history. There was a Viking with his horned hat, wielding a deadly ax. Next to him stood a woman dressed in a massive fur cloak, her mouth open in a shriek and holding a bow and arrow. Her face was covered with green tattoos. In front of her was a Japanese samurai, his deadly sword held above his head as if to strike.

Jack realized that the corridor was so long that he couldn't see the end — and it was lined with the wax dummies.

"Professor, who put them here?" he whispered.

The professor was silent for a moment, and Jack wondered if he didn't know the answer.

But the professor replied in an unusually subdued voice,

"They were once men and women, the greatest warriors of their people. They came down to the fairy kingdom to fight the fairy king. But they lost."

Jack felt his heart go cold. "But, Professor," he whispered, "why would the fairies make wax dummies of warriors who came to fight them?"

Sighing, the professor replied, "They aren't dummies, lad. They're stuffed."

Jack's eyes widened in horror. "But — but — people don't get stuffed!"

"The warriors were killed in battle against the fairies. Their dead bodies were stuffed as punishment for daring to try to fight them."

Jack stared. That would be him. Except, the dummies were lucky really. They were just dead. Gretel planned to turn him into a living statue, alive but trapped inside a stone shell. That was worse than death. Why was he bothering? Being killed and stuffed seemed almost kind compared to the fate Gretel had in store for him.

Because, he reluctantly thought, there was a chance he could save himself and many others as well — perhaps even hundreds of children. That was a gamble he realized that he was willing to take. Feeling slightly better, but no less frightened — well, terrified — Jack took a deep breath. He nodded at the professor.

They started to walk along the corridor. Ariel didn't like it and jumped into Jack's arms so he could carry her. She cuddled in close and stuck her head under his arm, to avoid the warriors' glassy, staring eyes.

Their footsteps made a hollow sound and left prints in the dust. *No one has walked this way for many years,* Jack thought.

A bright light lit the end of the corridor and they were momentarily dazed when they reached the end. Blinking, Jack realized they were in an enormous underground cavern, which was empty except for a massive fireplace carved into the rock. The fireplace was at least thirty feet long and twenty feet high. A roaring fire blazed in its depths, and two stone dragons sat on either side, their mouths open in ferocious snarls.

"Where is everyone?" Jack asked.

Jack and the professor walked into the room and stared. Jack found that he couldn't stop looking at the fireplace and the roaring flames. Frowning, he said, "Professor, it looks like there's something moving in the fire."

The professor began to advance toward it, but neither of them could get too close because of the heat. There did appear to be something moving, but Jack realized that it wasn't just something — it was many things.

The flames danced, spat, then turned luminous blue. Air rushed around the room. A muffled drum began to beat out a slow and deep rhythm from somewhere far away.

The professor whispered, "The fairy kingdom is on the move, lad."

The drumming beat out faster and faster.

Jack was about to ask what he meant when the blue flames whooshed into the room. They dove to the floor for cover, Jack shielding Ariel with his arms.

Hundreds of tiny flying figures burst from the fireplace, carried by the blue flames. They swarmed in and covered the ceiling, screeching in a high-pitched language that hurt human ears.

Ariel began to yowl and Jack felt like joining in. The fairies were a horrible sight.

They zoomed above their heads. Jack could see the fairies looked nothing like the illustrations from children's books. They had pointed features and skin the color of green moss. Tiny red eyes glared at Jack and the professor, and their bows were strung with spiderwebs. The arrows seemed to be made of black wasp stingers, and hundreds of them were pointed at Jack and the professor.

The fairies hovered in the air for a few seconds, then moved like a black cloud toward one end of the room. They used their bodies to form the shape of a throne, and one fairy, slighter bigger than the others, sat on top of the makeshift throne.

"Behold the fairy king," the professor gasped.

The fairy king wore a crown of dead moths and a tunic made of winter leaves. His eyes were cold beneath the crown. He stared at Jack and the professor.

"Who dares to enter our kingdom?" he squealed.

Jack took a deep breath and walked in front of the professor, gently dropping Ariel to the floor. He walked as close to the throne as he dared, feeling thousands of evil eyes staring at him.

The fairy king gave a cruel laugh and said, "You! You are the most pitiful of all the warriors so far!" Frowning, he continued, "Where is your armor? Where are your magical weapons? You would not dare to mock us, coming to fight the fairy kingdom without a single blade."

"It's just me, um, Jack Riddle," Jack replied, feeling his face flush.

The fairies began to yammer in their strange language. Jack couldn't tell what they were saying but supposed it wasn't good.

"Silence!" cried the fairy king. Immediately, the fairies were quiet. The fairy king glared furiously at Jack.

Beads of sweat began to trickle down Jack's forehead, but he maintained eye contact with the fairy king. He somehow knew that if he were to look away, then he, the professor, and Ariel, would all be killed and stuffed.

The fire crackled in the background, and the king seemed to make up his mind about something. With a snort, he drummed his fingers on one skinny knee and said, "Very well, Jack-of-the-Riddle, I'm curious. And it's been many years since I felt curious about anything!" He leaned forward. "Why are you here, teeny tiny human-child, if not to fight us for our magic?"

The professor whispered, "You need to tell him the absolute truth, because he can sniff out any lies you might speak. Just tell him we need his advice on how to fulfill the prophecy."

Jack gulped and walked up to the foot of the throne. After taking a big, shuddering breath, he told the listening fairies the whole story — from when he arrived at Gretel's house to her attempt to catch him on the train that very day.

The king listened, nodding his head from time to time and grunting in what Jack hoped was sympathy. He also wore the same avid expression that Jack had seen many times on the professor's face, which was unsettling to see mirrored on the fairy's strange features.

Finally, the king held up one hand and barked, "I have heard enough." He stood and flew off his throne. The fairies broke apart and settled around him in the air once more.

"You are lucky, human-child, that we are not very fond of Gretel. She stole the wand from a woman we had given it to, a woman who was deserving of such power — for a human. Humph. She was pure of heart, which meant there was a balance in the universe. Her goodness and our mischief meant harmony within the world. Dark cannot exist without light," he added, absentmindedly.

Jack thought that made a kind of sense, but he was still surprised the fairies cared about things like balancing out all the good and evil in the world.

The professor didn't look surprised. He smiled eagerly. "Does that mean you will tell us what the last part of the prophecy means?"

All the fairies began to giggle. The sound bounced around the cave and made it feel as if the whole Earth was laughing. Jack's skin crawled at the sound.

"Why, there is no fun in just telling you, human-man!" the fairy king chortled. "We have been asleep these past hundred years or more. We want some entertainment!"

The fairies laughed even harder. Jack felt his heart sink. For a wonderful moment he had thought it would be that easy. The fairies obviously didn't like Gretel, so why shouldn't they want to destroy her? But the white witch had warned him of the fairies' evil nature. She had said they were not to be trusted.

The fairy king clapped his hands. The strange sound of moving stone filled the cave. Before Jack could turn to see where the sound was coming from, the king began to speak.

"Your name has inspired me, human-child!"

Jack wasn't sure he liked the sound of that.

"Let's see if you can live up to your name. Fiddle-dee-dee, riddle me!" he cried.

Jack had a nasty feeling he knew where this was going.

"I will tell you a riddle. And, if you answer correctly, I will give you a gift — the element of fire."

Jack gasped. The second part of the prophecy mentioned fire. They had to bring fire with water and spirit to the place where earth and air meets. Jack had repeated the prophecy so many times that he knew it by heart.

The strange grinding sound started to grow louder. Although Jack hadn't turned around, he thought it was coming from the fireplace. The fairies flew toward it over his head, humming several notes over and over.

"Da, dee, da, FA FO FUM!" the fairies sang.

The fairy king hovered in the air and rubbed his hands together in glee. He leaned back and stared into the air above him. "Fiddle-dee-dee, RIDDLE ME!"

"Da, dee, da, FA FO FUM!" the fairies replied.

"Fiddle-dee-dee, RIDDLE ME!"

Somewhere, a deep drumming sound began again. The fairies continued to sing. The drumming grew faster. Their shouts grew louder.

The ground shuddered, and dust started to fall from the ceiling.

"It's a spell!" cried the professor. "It's a spell to wake one of the statues!" Sure enough, one of the statues by the fireplace had started to creak backward and forward. Jack and the professor spun around and realized with dread that one of the snarling stone dragons was starting to move.

CHAPTER 21
THE RIDDLE

"FIDDLE-DEE-DEE, RIDDLE ME!"

"Aaaa-deee-DAA-DEE-FAAAAA-FO-FUUUUUM!" the fairies howled.

No, Jack thought. *Anything but the dragon.* It had to be about the size of a bus.

But the dragon was shaking its head from side to side. The grinding sound grew louder. The fairies' humming increased so it could be heard over the shrieking of ancient stones.

"FA FO FUM!" they screamed, "FA-FO-FUM!"

The fairy king clapped his hands, and the singing and drumming stopped. A terrifying silence filled the cave.

Jack could feel his heart thudding in his ears.

Suddenly a roar of deadly fire belched from the dragon's lips. It rocked back and forth, flexing its clawed feet. Scaly skin burst through the stone, which cracked and fell. Jack and the professor shouted out in terror as the rocks tumbled to the floor, crashing down the walls and showering over their heads.

With great effort, the dragon pulled itself from the wall, shaking the last of the dust from its skin. It stalked into the middle of the cave, snorting white-hot flames.

Jack and the professor hurriedly backed away to the corner of the cave. Ariel had already sensibly taken cover in a tiny crack in the cave wall.

The king flew in front of Jack and pointed at him. "You, human-child, will entertain us. I will tell you a riddle, and you have to tell me the answer. You only get three guesses before you lose."

"Uh, that sounds OK."

Grinning, the fairy king added, "Well, you have to fight the dragon at the same time, of course."

The professor strode forward, shouting, "That's preposterous! He's only a child, and he hasn't got any weapons. You can't expect that!" Turning to Jack, he said, "There's only one thing that can defeat a dragon. You just have to —"

The king clicked his fingers. One of the fairies instantly fired an arrow at the professor.

Waaaaapppp! The arrow sank into his lip and stapled his mouth together. The professor clawed at his face, but couldn't dislodge the arrow or speak at all. Another fairy fired a tiny net that spun through the air, getting larger and larger. It fell over the professor, binding his arms and his legs tightly to his sides so he couldn't move.

"Oh, do pipe down, Ambrosius," the fairy king said, flapping his hand. "The boy will be fine! If not, well, there's plenty more human-child thingamabobs running around in the world." He shrugged. "I'm sure you can find a better specimen to give to his parents to replace this one. Looks a bit puny, anyway."

Just as Jack was trying to decide whether to be outraged or not, the fairies all took to the air and flew behind his back. Thousands of tiny hands then pushed him toward the waiting dragon.

The dragon lifted its head and roared at Jack, spitting flames from its mouth and nose. Jack tried desperately to move away, but the fairies kept pushing him toward the center of the cave.

"Professor," he shouted, "this would be a great time to explain how you kill a dragon!"

But the professor still couldn't speak or move. He could only wiggle up and down desperately as Jack was thrust in front of the drooling monster.

The fairy king clapped his hands and the fairies flew back to the other end of the cave, leaving Jack alone to face the dragon. It lowered its head and snuffed the air, making a damp, sucking sound.

Laughing, the king said, "Don't worry too much, little human-child — being scorched by a dragon is at least fast. It's either face the dragon and give yourself a chance . . . or refuse and I'll have my soldiers shoot you to death with our poisoned

arrows. Then we'll stuff you. You'd make a lovely footstool."
He grinned. "Which is it to be?" He paused. "Actually, I'm not
going to give you a choice, but never mind, it sounded very
impressive."

"Thanks a lot," Jack muttered. He drew a deep breath.
He couldn't figure out why the professor had taken him to
face the fairies. They were just as bad as Gretel. He felt his
confidence draining away. So what if he could drag himself
onto the top of a speeding train? There was no way he could
defeat a ten-ton dragon!

To make matters worse, the dragon was lumbering
toward Jack. Yellow, decayed fangs stuck out from its mouth,
and drool dripped onto the floor at its feet. The dragon
looked hungry.

Inching back, Jack listened to the fairy king recite the
riddle he had to solve.

"This is one of my favorite riddles, boy, but it is rather
tricky. If you solve it in three guesses, I'll call off the dragon
and give you something you need to fulfill the prophecy.

I have arms and legs, but cannot move,
I am alive, but many do not believe I live,
If untouched, I will be immortal to your mind,
But if cut by a blade, I am powerless to fight for life.
What am I?"

Jack gasped — he had absolutely no idea what the answer
was. He had hoped to at least have a good guess, but this was
impossible. As if on cue, the dragon chose this moment to

lunge forward, breathing flames. It struck like a cobra, fast and deadly. Jack shouted and dove to the ground, rolling to one side. Luckily, the flames missed him by an inch. Scrambling to his feet, he cried, "I don't know the answer, it's too hard — give me another one, please!"

The dragon roared and began to lumber after Jack, following him as he ran to the edge of the cave.

Laughing, the king replied, "Now that's not fair at all — you agreed to the terms when you entered my kingdom. Guess!"

The fairies all took up the chant, singing, "Guess, human-child, guess! Guess, human-child, guess!"

Another flame whizzed past Jack's ear as he ran and he ducked, swerving to the right. The dragon was slow and couldn't keep up with Jack. But he knew he couldn't outrun it in a circular cave. Eventually he would tire and the dragon would cook him, then eat him — hopefully in that order.

As his legs pounded the floor, Jack thought furiously. *What has arms and legs but can't move, and is alive-ish?*

A claw darted into his vision, and Jack realized the dragon had managed to catch up with him. With a yell, he tried to dodge the claw but was too late. Instead of taking off half his face, it missed and racked his ribs instead. The pain was blinding, making him gasp and stagger.

But still Jack raced on, going faster in a desperate attempt to outrun the dragon again.

The professor managed to jump up and down on the spot. "Ummmmmmpphhhiiiiinnnnn!"

The fairies had all cheered when the dragon clawed Jack and shouted even more when they saw the blood dripping from his side onto the ground.

Jack tried to ignore them and concentrate again on the riddle. He thought furiously, struggling to come up with anything that could be alive but sort of not at the same time. He remembered a film he'd seen a few weeks ago, which felt like a lifetime ago. It had been set in the future and had robots in it. Suddenly he thought he knew the answer. "It's a robot!" he shouted. "R-r-robots are immortal unless we turn them off! A-a-and they have arms and l-l-legs too!"

Jack slowed his pace and grasped his side, sure he was right and that the fairies would call off the dragon.

But the fairy king replied, "Now why would I choose a robot as the answer? What are human inventions to me? That doesn't help you at all — and, really, Jack, you know that proper robots don't exist! Human stuff and nonsense." Rubbing his hands together with glee, he said, "Two guesses left!"

No, Jack thought, *I can't keep running.* He started off again, but the dragon had caught up with him when he had slowed down to shout out his guess.

Strangely, the one thought that filled his head was that the fairy king had started to sound a lot like the professor when he became irritated. He realized he had to keep his mind on the riddle to survive, but for some reason he couldn't stop thinking about the odd similarities between them.

A mewling sound reached Jack's ears as he kept dodging the dragon's flames. He risked turning his head to look. Ariel had crawled out of her hiding place and was sitting below the king, meowing furiously at him.

The king seemed to understand her. He nodded his head and said, "Ah, but fish-lady, surely you won't begrudge us a bit of fun? Oh, I understand he's quite important and all that, but isn't it so entertaining to see him run and run and RUN? No? Really? What do you mean, balance? I am ALWAYS fair."

Ariel arched her back and hissed at the king, who sighed. "Fine. A small weapon may help even the odds a bit, to make it more sporting. But only because it's you, Ariel."

The fairy king clicked his fingers, and a sword appeared in Jack's hand. Jack gasped in surprise. It was small and fit his palm perfectly. The blade was rusted, but it was still wickedly sharp. The hilt had a blazing sun carved into it, the rays twisted with crystals. Jack wrapped both hands tightly around the handle. But what was he to do with it? Sharp as it was, it couldn't do much against a ten-ton dragon that could use it as a toothpick.

But Jack was tiring, and the blood loss was making him dizzy. It dripped form his wound and was weakening him with every step, making his legs feel like jelly. He knew he couldn't carry on running anymore.

Screwing his eyes shut and gathering all his courage, Jack

turned and faced the dragon, which was approaching again. He pointed the sword at the dragon and thought that at least he had a small chance.

To Jack's amazement, a flash of brilliant blue light flew from the tip of the sword into the dragon's eyes. Jack covered his face with his hands . The light was so intense that it momentarily blinded him.

The dragon made a shrieking noise like a rusty garage door being opened and shook its head, trying to clear its eyes.

Jack drew a shuddering gasp and thought that the light had probably bought him a few minutes before it wore off and the dragon could see again.

Staggering as far away as he could from the roaring monster, he fell over and sat shakily on the ground. He glanced at the professor, who was still jumping up and down on the spot. He had managed to work his arms free of the net and was waving them madly. Jack frowned. The professor was obviously trying to tell him something, but he had no idea what it was.

The professor pointed to each of his arms, and then stood stock-still, with each arm held out in the air.

Nope, Jack thought, *not a clue.*

Desperately, he looked at the fairy king, who stared steadily back at him from under his crown of dead moths.

Jack decided to try to make another guess. "What about a germ?" he said wildly. "It lives, but people never used to believe in them. They live forever unless you get medicine to kill them and make you better."

For a wonderful second, Jack thought it was the right answer. The fairies all hummed, and the king smiled.

The professor groaned and slapped his forehead.

Jack's smile faltered. *Uh-oh,* he thought.

"Human-child, you are wrong." Gleefully, the king continued, "Only one more guess before my friend here cooks you. He is feeling much better, by the way." He gestured to the spot just in front of Jack.

Jack slowly raised his eyes. There, not ten feet away, stood the dragon. Its eyes were bloodshot, and it was panting, drool dripping on the ground. It was furious.

Jack tried to pull himself to his feet, but the wound in his side was too painful. He was exhausted and fell forward to his knees in front of the dragon.

He raised the sword to blind it again, but the dragon roared a jet of fire toward Jack. He cringed and screwed his eyes shut, waiting for the flames to burn his skin off. But the pain never came. Jack opened his eyes and saw that the flames were somehow flowing around him. They were bouncing off the sword and running harmlessly around his body.

The dragon gave a frustrated roar. Breathing spirals of fire, it began to advance toward Jack. The ground shuddered with every step it took.

The professor was practically spinning on the spot, trying to make Jack see the answer.

The fairy king turned to the professor and said, "Not a very good riddler, is he, Ambrosius?"

Glaring, the professor carried on gesturing to his arms and bound feet.

In a far corner of his mind, Jack wondered how the king knew the professor's first name.

But Jack was too tired to think. His mind slowed even more with terror when he realized the dragon was getting closer.

He felt strangely dreamy. *So this is how I die. Funny. I didn't expect this. It'll sound quite impressive on my tombstone, though — death by dragon.* Everything in the room fell away as if it didn't exist.

The fairies had started to cheer on the dragon, which lumbered toward him, but Jack could barely hear them.

A vision of an ancient tree suddenly floated in front of his eyes. It was the most beautiful thing he had ever seen in his life. *Perhaps it's a sort of tree of life you only see when you die,* he thought. He'd read that in religious education class at school. He wondered what trees saw when they died. How funny if they saw a human instead. *But no*, he chided himself, *trees don't really live, although I suppose . . .* His heart skipped a beat, and the dreamy sensation shattered.

"It's a tree!" Jack cried desperately. The dragon froze and the fairies stopped cheering.

"The answer to the riddle is a tree," Jack babbled. "It has branches and roots, like arms and legs, but it can't move. And, um, we don't think they're alive like we are, and unless we cut them down, they live for hundreds of years. That's kind of immortal to us!" Jack was triumphant. He knew somehow, deep down, that this was the real answer.

The fairy king's face screwed up into a scowl. Jack watched in fascination as real steam began to pour from his ears. The king clenched his hands into fists and shouted, "Nooooo! No, no, no, no! No one has ever solved that riddle before." He flew over to Jack and hovered in front of his face, shouting, "You cheated! Somehow you cheated!"

Jack grinned and clutched his bleeding side. "How'd I cheat?"

The fairy king opened his mouth but couldn't think of any answer.

The professor finally managed to pull off the last of the net from his legs and jogged over to Jack, silently punching the air with joy. Jack laughed, thinking of what the professor would normally be saying at this moment.

The king started to fly in loop-de-loops, screaming his anger. The fairies all joined in, zooming through the air, tearing at their hair and scratching their cheeks to draw blood.

Finally the king slowed. He seemed to realize he was beaten. He gestured impatiently toward the dragon, which blasted up into the air like a small rocket and back toward to fireplace, instantly stiffening, growing pale and turning back into stone.

The rest of the fairies flew over to them, glowering in

fury. They buzzed around their heads, sounding like a hive of killer wasps.

Ariel jumped up on the professor's shoulder and swiped at the arrow sticking out of his cheek. It fell to the floor, where the professor stamped on it. Clearing his throat, he croaked, "Thank you, Ariel, and thank you for requesting the Sword of Power for young Jack here. Without it, he'd be a piece of crispy toast!"

Ariel purred and twined herself around Jack's legs. Painfully, he stooped and picked her up. "How would you defeat a dragon, then?"

The professor looked blank for a moment then said, "Oh yes! It's surprisingly easy. You sing them a nursery rhyme!"

"Seriously?" Jack ducked as a particularly upset fairy zoomed too close to his head.

"Yes, they're very fond of 'Baa Baa Black Sheep.' Sends them straight to sleep."

They looked at each other, then burst into hysterical laughter.

The professor recovered first. "But you did very well! I'm awfully proud of you," he said awkwardly.

"Well," said the fairy king sarcastically, "as lovely as this little scene is, perhaps you would like to be given your prize, so you can get out of my kingdom and stop filling it with your human stink, hmm?"

Warily, they nodded at him. The fairy king bared his teeth in what was meant to be a smile, then snapped his fingers.

The fireplace spluttered and a lump of coal shot out, zooming toward him.

He turned and held up his hand. The coal slowed, before landing neatly in his palm.

"Open your hand, ridiculously tiny human-child!" he ordered.

Jack gulped — surely the coal would burn the skin off his hand? He turned to the professor, who just nodded his head encouragingly. Trembling, Jack held out his hand and waited for the hot coal to sizzle through his skin and pop it like a sausage.

The king dropped the coal into Jack's hand. Jack yelped, but not because it was hot — it was cold. About the size of a penny, it seemed to be made of black crystal. A tiny red flame flickered inside the crystal.

The fairy king said, "This is the first coal we gave to humankind thousands of years ago." He shrugged. "We gave humans fire, because without it they would have died out. And we were so bored. Humans are such fun to play tricks on."

The professor just nodded again and then gently pulled Jack to his feet and toward the entrance of the cave. "We can go, boy — the fairies have had their fun, and we got what we came for. Time to go home."

The fairies started to laugh, the sound echoing through the cave. "We're never done with you once you've visited us of your own free will!" shouted the fairy king. He flew back to the rest of the fairies, who were moving back toward the fireplace. "Remember that, Ambrosius — we will meet again soon! We always do!"

In a flash of blue fire, the fairies were swallowed by the eerie flames. They disappeared inside the stone fireplace to sleep once more.

* * *

Their little group walked slowly back through the tunnel, Jack limping in pain. The professor almost had to carry him the last few steps. At the end, they found an old cart with a frayed rope. When they pulled on the rope, it hoisted itself up the chute they had fallen through earlier. Finally, after much cursing, the professor managed to pull them all up to the top. He then muttered a short sentence in a language Jack didn't understand. The professor pushed with all his strength on the stone lid, which flipped over, revealing daylight.

Smash grinned down at them, blocking out the light. Jack had never been so glad to see his ugly face.

CHAPTER 22

THE CONFESSION

When Jack awoke the next morning, every bone in his body ached as though a giant had battered him with a hammer. He was ridiculously happy to be alive. The sun streamed through the bedroom window, illuminating Smash and Ariel. They were lying at the end of the bed, snoring loudly. But things hadn't been so peaceful when he'd arrived home the night before.

When he had walked through the front door, battered and bleeding, his mother had taken one look at him and shrieked like a banshee. The thought of it still made him wince. Grabbing him by one ear, she had marched him to the bathroom before scrubbing off every inch of soot and mud and taking half his skin off while she was at it. Ranting about how boys who fight in the streets plainly don't want their dinner, she had roughly bandaged him up — and sent him straight to bed.

Later though, Jack had heard his father's footsteps padding softly to the kitchen, then the creak of the floorboards. Soon there was a small chinking sound outside Jack's room. Confused, Jack had opened the door to find a tray containing a glass of orange juice, a plate of ginger cookies, and a thick beef sandwich.

Jack's eyes had stung.

Once he had eaten every scrap of food and licked the plate, Jack had collapsed on his bed and immediately fallen into a deep sleep. To his relief, he'd had no nightmares involving witches, fairies, or dragons.

The professor had said he was going to investigate any more myths that could be of help in finally understanding how to fulfill the prophecy spoken by the white witch on the gallows. *We seem to be so close,* thought Jack as he jumped out of bed, *but still so far from knowing what she meant.* His eyes focused on the windowsill.

Jack had placed the fairy king's coal on his window ledge last night before falling asleep. It gave off the same flickering light as it had the day before, and when he picked it up, it was still cold to the touch. Thoughtfully, he tossed it into the air and caught it.

"What are you?" he wondered.

Ariel interrupted at this moment by biting his ankle.

"Ouch! That does hurt, you know."

Jack's shout woke Smash, who leaped to his feet,

making the tarnished bells chime softly. "Breeekkkkiiieee nnnnnooooowwww." He burped.

"Nice! Good to see that being in terrible danger and shooting cans of soda at your mortal enemy — oh, and sister — then being chased by a group of angry tourists hasn't spoiled your appetite."

Smash grinned, showing razor-sharp teeth, and toddled out of the door and downstairs for his "brekkie."

After getting dressed, Jack followed him downstairs. His mom had gone out for an early shift, but his dad was sitting at the kitchen table. To Jack's astonishment, his dad appeared nervous.

"Would you come and sit down, Jack?" he asked, somewhat formally.

"Sure," Jack replied warily. He padded over to the table. Smash made his way to the fridge, jumped up to open the door, then swung from the handle as he considered the contents. He grabbed a bottle of chocolate milk and leaped to the floor. He opened a cupboard and pulled out a box of cereal. Stopping only to grab an enormous wooden spoon, the goblin waddled to his high chair.

Smash climbed in, poured all the chocolate milk into the cereal box and started to guzzle his breakfast.

Jack and his dad began to laugh as they were sprayed with bits of flying cereal.

Looking more relaxed, Mr. Riddle said, "Great idea

bringing that monkey into the house. Your mother really likes having him around."

Jack grinned and swung his legs under the table.

But Mr. Riddle frowned and examined his hands. There was a piece of burnt toast in front of him, which Jack thought was unusual. His dad never burned food.

"I wanted to talk to you. Properly." He looked up.

Jack swallowed, wondering if he was going to get another lecture on how he was messing up his life.

"I know we don't always agree on things," Mr. Riddle continued carefully. "But I had a chat with your mother the other night, and we agreed that I might be, perhaps, a bit too hard on you. Sometimes."

Jack wasn't sure what to say. He hated talking about this kind of stuff. A week ago, he would have murmured something like "no worries" and slunk away from the table. But now he felt he had a bit more courage.

"Maybe. Well, yeah. You are," he said firmly. "Sometimes I don't get why you keep telling me off about school. I'm actually all right at most subjects, you know."

Raising his eyebrows in surprise, Mr. Riddle said, "OK. We agree. Um, so, I suppose the reason is because I didn't do that well in school. I didn't take it seriously, to be honest. Failed all my core exams, like English and math. And don't get me wrong, I love my job — but it took me a really long time to get trained. You don't have many options if you flunk out. So I worry that'll happen to you. But if you want to spend more time doing history projects — or any other subject that you really like — then I won't say anything about it." He folded his arms. "Me and your mother both think it's important that you do what you enjoy."

"Great. Thanks," Jack said, his ears pink. "Can I get a new phone too?"

"Don't push it, lad." Mr. Riddle smiled.

* * *

After breakfast, Jack raced upstairs to get ready. Normally he would head to the local park with his friends on a Saturday, but he was going to visit the professor instead. He put Smash in his backpack (it only took ten minutes of shoving, followed by bribery using chocolate bars) and started off toward the professor's house on his bike, with Ariel trotting next to him. The professor had given him a map. After several wrong turns, Jack finally reached the right street.

The professor only lived a few miles away, but it seemed like a different city. It was gloomy, and the streets were covered in litter. Glass from broken shop windows and telephone booths lay in glittering heaps on the ground, so Jack had to swerve around them to avoid getting a flat tire. Once he found the house, he padlocked his bike to the railing and went to knock on the door.

Ariel mewed uncertainly. But Jack knew this was the right address. He walked up to the house. The paint on the front door was peeling. The house was set back from the main street and smelled a bit like wet dog.

Jack knocked and the door swung open.

The professor beamed. "Come in, come in! How are you, m'boy? Feeling better after your, er, scrape with the supernatural the other day? Yes? Excellent!"

Jack followed the professor into the house. Although outside it was dingy and gray, inside the house was cheerful and full of warmth. Books lined all available walls and surfaces, and the rich smell of their leather bindings filled the air. A log fire crackled in the living room, where there were several comfy-looking leather armchairs. A brass skillet full of pine cones lay next to the fire, and the professor leaned down to throw a few of the biggest ones into the fire. The heady smell of Christmas pine needles filled the room as they burned.

"Do please sit down, all of you," the professor said. Jack took one of the battered armchairs. Ariel curled up in front of the fire, purring, and Smash peeked out from the top of the backpack. He seemed happy to stay inside the bag for the time being, although Jack had no idea why.

The professor went into his tiny kitchen, where a whistling kettle was boiling. He filled two large mugs, added tea bags and milk, then carried them through.

Jack settled back with his tea. "So, professor, have you found anything new?"

There was a slight pause. "Well, I think it's about time I told you a few facts that I've, ahem, kept quiet about until this moment."

Jack didn't have a clue what to say. He had almost been expecting this, ever since the fairy king had seemed to know the professor.

The professor stared at Jack. His lower lip began to tremble, and he looked for all the world like he was about to start crying.

Hastily, Jack tried to reassure him. "It's OK, just tell me quickly. I'm sure it can't be that bad. Can it?"

"Well, m'boy, it can be. You see, I'm a bit tiny older than I look." Pause. "By about two thousand years. Give or take a decade."

"You're HOW OLD?" Jack cried, nearly spilling hot tea on his lap.

"I didn't really want to, well, overload you with too much information when we first started this quest."

From inside the backpack, Smash snorted with laughter. "Chaaaatter, chatter, chatterbox!"

Smiling slightly, the professor continued, "Perhaps compared to what I've already told you, it wouldn't have been too much of a leap. And yes," he said, addressing the backpack, "I do have a tendency to talk too much!"

"Come on, Professor!" Jack said. "What else have you been keeping from me? It's not as if I can't take it by now. I think."

Remembering back to when he had taken the train to Gretel's house, Jack marveled at how far he had come. It felt as though his life before then had been seen through a spectrum of gray. Everything had been so normal and, well, boring. But even though he was now fighting for his life, the world seemed more alive — and dangerous. He remembered Gretel's empty eye socket streaming blood. She would never forgive him for that.

With a shiver, Jack turned his attention back to the professor, who still had a slight smile on his face.

"Jack, Jack," he said. "You've done so well, m'boy. You have seen and stood against forces of darkness that people haven't faced for hundreds of years." He paused and stared down at his cup of tea. "But I couldn't tell you who I really was. You might not have trusted me. And rightly so. My reputation is a bit, shall we say, tarnished. In my defense, I was a man of my time. What you would consider immoral behavior these days, like helping to start wars and such, was pretty normal in my time. Life was cheaper then."

Silence. Jack was dumbfounded.

Ariel mewed, and the professor reached down to scratch behind her ears. He whispered, "I was once a very powerful man. Mighty kings and queens would come to me and beg for my wisdom. A word from me and their kingdoms would rise or fall, taking all their people with them. I was the greatest and most respected magician this world has ever seen."

Jack stared at the professor in dismay. *Perhaps the fight with the fairy king has scrambled the professor's brain,* he thought.

Sitting in an old armchair, the professor could not have

seemed less like the mightiest magician in the world. His shoulders were hunched, his gray hair was wild, and his clothes were shabby.

"You don't have to say it, Jack. I recognize what you are thinking. Has the old man finally gone off his rocker?"

Jack blushed and wished he had never started this conversation. He felt awful doubting the professor, who had been his only friend and protector (not counting Smash and Ariel, he mentally corrected). But really, what was he meant to think?

"Things are rarely as they seem, Jack, especially in this world where evil lurks under dripping stones and dark waters." Standing, the professor took off his glasses and stared hard at Jack. "What you see before you is a broken-down old man. My fate was so awful that it turned me from the powerful being I was into this shell. My real name is Ambrosius Merlin."

CHAPTER 23
BETRAYAL

"You're WHO?" yelled Jack. He couldn't take it in. He knew bits and pieces about the legend of Merlin, but only from movies about King Arthur and Camelot.

The professor started to wring his hands.

"You have to understand that if I had told you before, you wouldn't have believed me! And you may not really trust me now that you know who I really am. But that meddling old fairy king dropped such a big hint, I knew you'd figure it out eventually."

"Uh, no, I probably wouldn't have," Jack said honestly.

The professor ignored him and started to pace round the room, still with his teacup in his hand, then whirled to face Jack, spraying cold tea on the floor.

"I knew I had to tell you as soon as possible. There can't be anymore secrets between us, Jack. We have to trust each other if we're going to vanquish Gretel. And we're so close!

Close to stopping her hideous games that have gone on for generations!"

"OK, OK, calm down, Professor! Uh, do you still want me to call you that?"

The professor hesitated. Then suddenly, he started to laugh. Great gales of laughter, until he was almost doubled up on the floor.

"It wasn't that funny, you know," Jack said indignantly.

"I'm sorry," wheezed the professor, wiping tears of laughter from his eyes. "It's just that no one has asked me that in years. Sometimes I even forget my own name! Oh, ha-ha!"

Impatiently, Ariel ran over to the professor and bit him sharply on the ankle.

"Ouch! If you weren't already enchanted, I would have used one of my last pieces of magic to turn you into something equally horrible for that."

Ariel hissed and curled into a ball at Jack's feet.

Still muttering under his breath, the professor strode from the room.

"Great," Jack said, looking down at the cat, "that wasn't very helpful, was it?"

Ariel flicked her tail over her face in reply and promptly went to sleep.

Jack heard footsteps above him and then an almighty crash. He jumped, but Ariel carried on snoozing. He realized that the professor was searching for something. And, by the sound of it, turning half his house upside down in the process.

After a few minutes, the professor ran down the stairs, two at a time. "This," he shouted, "is a piece of my old magic!"

In his hand was a ball of light. It glowed like a tiny sun and was impossible to look at directly. Jack tried to shield his eyes, but the light burned through his hand. It filled the room with a dancing, crystal shimmer. It was beautiful, powerful — and terrifying.

"Turn it down," Jack pleaded, "or I'm gonna go blind!" Jack could feel the nerves in his eyes beginning to burn as red lights flashed across the darkness behind his eyelids.

"Oops!" The professor hastily covered the ball with a lace doily from the table. Instantly, the light softened, although Jack could still see it pulsing through the professor's hand.

"Sorry, m'boy, I got a bit carried away. Forgot that mortals have a hard time looking at raw magic."

Scowling, Jack uncovered his eyes.

"Strangely, lace can veil magic. Odd, that — I never worked out why. Best thing for it."

The professor moved into the room and sat back in his armchair. Gingerly, he transferred the glowing ball of light onto the coffee table between the two of them.

"I used to have a cave full of this raw magic," mused the professor, "all powerful and all my own. No one could have stopped me — certainly not that amateur Gretel."

"So what happened?" asked Jack.

The professor's face became stern. Suddenly Jack thought he could see how he used to be. It was as though the face of the kind, bumbling old man was masking the real person underneath. Jack could see the outline of a strong, harsh profile. The eyes were hard, glittering. It was someone Jack very much hoped he would never have to meet.

Hastily, he said, "Professor, I think you're fine the way you are. Perhaps it's a good thing you had to become more, um, normal? A bit less all powerful and scary?"

A sweet smile from the older man broke the moment. The second personality seemed to disappear, and he looked once more like Jack's friend.

"That's very nice of you, Jack. I doubt we would have gotten along so well if you had known me before I lost my magic."

He dropped his gaze to the glowing ball on the table. "My name was Merlin, and I was born into a poor family, two thousand years ago. I was a sickly child, and my parents immediately realized that I would be a burden to them, because I wouldn't grow up strong and be able to work. Times were harder then, and if you couldn't work, you wouldn't survive. So they left me under a willow tree that the fairies were known to haunt. They left me there as a gift, hoping I would be taken into the fairy world and return stronger. Or just freeze to death."

Jack shuddered. He couldn't decide which was worse.

The thought of growing up in the fairy world was horrible. No sunlight, no love, no kindness — only the endless spiteful laughter of the fairy folk.

The professor nodded grimly. "I was lucky, although some people wouldn't say that. The fairies did take me away. I never saw my real parents again. I won't frighten you with tales of my life there, but I will say that it was not pleasant."

Here the professor swallowed hard. He appeared to be years older at that moment, as the memories came back.

"Anyway, the good news is, I managed to escape when I was fifteen years old. And when I escaped, I took with me all the knowledge of the fairy folk. Plus an ancient map to a lost cave that contained a store of raw magic."

The professor ran his hands carefully over the glowing ball on the coffee table.

"Raw magic is what shapes the world, m'boy. It can be made into anything you wish, and it can do anything you want. It is extremely dangerous because it can be used to create — or to destroy. You have a choice.

"I decided to make myself into the most powerful magician the world had ever seen. My reputation grew over hundreds of years, and my immense and terrible wisdom and power were sought by the greatest legends of the world. King Arthur himself was one of my pupils. But then it all went wrong. The fairies decided to go on the move and visit Earth."

Jack imagined he could hear the muffled beat of a

faraway drum and see the fairies swarming from their home in the blue fire to find the professor.

"Yes," he continued, "they came to find me and claim the magic as their own. It was their right, but I still fought them. There was a long, painful battle, during which we scorched the countryside and many people were killed. But I lost. They imprisoned me in the cave for a thousand years as my punishment."

"What happened when you got out? How did you get out?" Jack breathed.

"I managed to escape with the help of a strange and ancient creature that guards the caves to the underworld. It has no name, but it's very dangerous. The creature is made of shadows, talons, claws, and teeth. It can take you to any fantastic and strange world you want to visit, but there's a price to be paid."

The professor paused. "Anyway, that's a story for another day. When I finally got out, Gretel was waiting for me. She had heard all the stories about me and decided to see for herself. But she couldn't afford to have such a rival. Even without the cave full of magic, I still knew too much and could always find another magical store hidden somewhere in the lost parts of the world. She knew that I would easily kill her, prophecy or no prophecy. It would be like stepping on an insect to me."

The cold way in which the professor said this made Jack's blood freeze. Where had the nice teacher gone? Had this man always been underneath? Sure, he wanted to stop Gretel as well. But Jack could never think about her as an insect to be squashed — it was too inhuman.

"So, Gretel disguised herself as a snake and went to the cave when I woke up. She enchanted me when I was still weak from my long sleep. She cursed me. And her curse was the worst I could have ever imagined. Not even the fairy king, with his love of evil pranks, would have stooped so low."

He spread his hands and gazed at Jack in despair.

"She made me an object of scorn. She turned me into this bumbling man you see today. Her curse was that, no matter what I said, no one would ever believe me. She wiped my memory of any knowledge that might lead me to another store of magic. She also wiped my memory of almost all the spells I had ever learned, leaving me with just frustrating bits and pieces of fragments that I can never quite remember. So, you see, she left me with no way to find more magic, no way to cast any spells, and no way for anyone to ever believe another word I said."

Jack was lost for words. But there was more to come.

The professor picked up the glowing ball of magic and said, "This is the final chapter of our journey, m'boy. Do you have the mermaid's vial and the fairies' coal?"

Jack nodded. The vial was still around his neck, and the coal was in the backpack with Smash. He trusted the goblin to keep it safe for him. But, he wasn't so sure he still trusted the professor. He'd told him who he really was, but only because he thought Jack would work it out.

"Excellent, then let's begin." The professor started to wave his hand over the ball.

"Wait, WHAT? Hang on!" Jack leaped up from his chair and began to back away.

Frowning, the professor said, "What's wrong, Jack? Surely you want all this to be over?"

"But Professor," he protested. "I don't have a clue what you're about to do and, worse, I don't really know who you are anymore. And that thing looks seriously dangerous!"

A tiny jangle of bells alerted him to Smash's presence. He had crawled out of the backpack and was standing in front of Jack. He snarled at the professor.

With a sigh, the professor placed the ball of magic back on the table.

"Jack, Jack." He shook his head. "This is what we have been leading up to. I managed to keep hold of this small piece of magic, which you see on the table before you. I could have used it to create riches for myself or to give me a doorway to another world where things might be easier for me. But I didn't."

"Why?"

"Because, you thickheaded boy," he bellowed, "I was waiting for you to figure out how to fulfill the prophecy!"

Jack winced. "Bit harsh," he muttered.

"Stop looking like a cowardly sheep! Yes, you are clever enough, and no, it wasn't just luck that has helped you on your way to finding those elemental treasures."

Jack had to sit down. He was feeling faint. With a desperate laugh, he thought that if he was all that special, he wouldn't have such issues with staying conscious.

Ignoring Jack, the professor waved his hand over the ball again. "There is one spell that I remember. One spell that I said over and over again, even while Gretel was wiping my memory. I had to make sure I would never, ever forget, when the time came to use it. And that time is now!"

Jumping to his feet, Jack shouted, "Professor, stop! Whatever you're doing, just stop!"

But it was too late. The ball of magic began to whizz like a spinning top. The light grew brighter and burned off the lace doily. The ball rose above the professor's head. He was muttering some sort of spell in a low voice. The professor carefully raised his hands, and the ball gave off a flash of brilliant light.

Suddenly, Jack, Ariel, Smash, and the professor all rose into the air. Static crackled around them, and their hair stood on end.

"*Ohmygod, ohmygod*, what're you doing?" Jack yelled.

Then, with a mighty flash of light, the world dissolved around them.

CHAPTER 24

THE LEGEND OF JACK RIDDLE

They were falling fast into the dark.

Suddenly there was a bright white light surrounding them.

They were hurtling through a tunnel of light, traveling over the Earth.

Jack tried to scream, but they were going so fast that he couldn't draw enough breath.

Time passed.

Below them, outside the swirling tunnel, Jack could see the ocean. It was terrifyingly far down.

Falling.

Flying.

Endless.

Blinding light.

Then deepest darkness.

* * *

When Jack woke, it was twilight. With a groan, he sat up. The wound in his side had split open, and he could feel something sticky on his rib cage.

"It's you again, is it? Wowzarooney! I thought you'd be back. And you traveled using raw magic — ouch. That would be painful, that would."

Gasping, Jack opened his eyes. Standing in front of him was the tree guardian. It was the same creature he had persuaded to let him through the doorway in the tree, so he could follow Gretel into the Lost Forest where she kept her carousel cauldron.

The tree guardian was looking at Jack with concern. He noticed for the first time that, underneath the hundreds of wrinkles, he had split pupils like Gretel, but they were kind.

"Up you get, master. You'll need your strength to face her." The guardian yanked Jack to his feet. Swaying slightly, Jack looked around and tried to get his bearings. Then he groaned. He was back in the glade where he had run for his life from Gretel and where he had met Ariel.

Whirling round, he realized that he didn't know where Ariel, the professor, or even Smash were. He stared around wildly and saw that they were scattered around him in a circle. They were still unconscious.

"As I said, it takes time to get used to such powerful magic. Raw, too, by the looks of it." The guardian gave a sniff. "'Course, you're tougher than that bunch. You're awake and they're still in dream land!" The guardian snorted with laughter and promptly tipped over.

The creature still had a long chain around its ankle, which led back to an enormous tree in the middle of the glade. He could go no further.

Seeing Jack's gaze, he nodded. "Aye, I'm trapped here. It's my fate to guard the doorways between worlds — and this makes sure I can never leave." He grinned. "But it's good to see you again, oh bard of the forest. Any chance of a few pops made of cocoa?" he asked hopefully.

Numbly, Jack shook his head. He couldn't think. Why were they here? Why had the professor pretty much kidnapped them and brought them back to where they might run into Gretel?

As if responding to these thoughts, the professor gave a gasp and sat up. His glasses had shattered, and he pulled them off his nose in disgust. "Pesky things; never did like them. Well, hopefully after this is all over I won't have such human frailties anymore." He looked up. "Jack, m'boy!"

Pulling himself to his feet, he started to walk over to Jack. Clapping his hands, he said, "Time to bring this story to a close, I think!"

The guardian studied Jack with fascination. He'd never seen a human go that shade of bright red before.

Jack was so angry he could feel it fizzing through his veins. All his pent-up frustrations were buzzing around in his head, which felt like it would explode.

The professor faltered when he saw Jack's face.

"You've put us all in danger!" Jack bellowed. "Do you even know where we are? This is Gretel's glade. This is where she cooks up her potions! We've walked right into the place where she's the strongest, with nothing to defend ourselves!"

Silence fell. The professor gaped, his mouth opening and closing like a stranded fish.

Ariel stirred. With a final glare at the professor, Jack walked over to check that she was OK. Mewling, she jumped onto his shoulder. With shaking hands, Jack gently stroked the top of her head. Purring, she wrapped herself around his neck.

Jack turned to see if Smash was awake, but the goblin had already toddled over to look at the tree in the center of the glade. He stood underneath it with his back to them all, the bells on his hat gently chiming in the wind. It was a lonely sound.

"Jack," the professor gasped. "I had to do it."

"Do what?" Jack demanded.

"I commanded the magic to take us to where we would face our final battle with Gretel — where the prophecy would be fulfilled. You're ready to beat her, I just know you are!" The professor looked at Jack with pleading eyes.

Then we're all dead, Jack thought, *because I still don't get how to fulfill it.*

Jack was so sunk in despair that he hadn't noticed the door to the tree slowly creaking open.

"Bard of the forest, fish-lady, and ancient man — run!" the guardian hissed. With a squeal, he ran back toward the tree. "Coming, mistress! Here I am!"

The guardian hurried inside the door and disappeared.

The professor turned back to Jack. He said urgently, "You can do this. Come on, the solution should be obvious to a clever boy like you now that we're here!" He gestured to the glade around them. "We have the elements with us! You've battled creatures that no other child has bested, and all you have to do is figure out the final piece of the puzzle!"

Jack shook his head in despair. "You've got it all wrong! I don't have a clue!"

"I saw how fighting the dragon made you think more quickly. All you need is a bit of pressure to help you crack it!" The professor patted his pocket. "And don't worry. I have a plan to buy us a little more time while you figure it out." He started to mutter something under his breath.

Then a shadow fell over them.

Gretel had arrived.

"Well, hello Jackie-poo." Gretel stepped out from the tree. She wore her usual ball gown, combat boots, and battered top hat. Her empty eye socket was covered with a black eye patch. She looked like a young girl on her way to a costume party.

But Jack knew better.

An eerie growling came from the head hidden under her hat. It sounded like a starving wolf — low, hungry, and sinister.

The professor was still muttering under his breath. Gretel

cast him a scornful glance. "You foolish old man," she said, her voice cutting through the air like a whip. "Did you really think that your meddling would make the slightest bit of difference?"

She was close now, only ten feet away. In a distant part of his mind, Jack realized that he hadn't seen Smash since he had wandered up to the tree. *Good,* he thought. *I hope he manages to get away.*

Gretel stared at the professor. "I got rid of your powers a hundred years ago when I put my spell on you. You're like a forgetful old dog with a muzzle, and yet you still try to interfere with my plans!

"However," she continued thoughtfully, tapping her teeth with her wand, "I feel I must thank you Merlin, for bringing me this tricky boy. He has a terrible habit of never quite behaving the way I expect him to. Funny that — I didn't expect him to get this far. Anyway, all's well that ends well. Here he is, ready to meet his destiny and become a story to warn the rest of his generation."

The hat had started to wobble from side to side and the growling grew deeper and louder. With a long-suffering sigh, Gretel pulled off her hat.

Her hideous mummified head glared down at them, its cracked and shriveled skin the color of old tea. It began to snarl, showing decayed teeth.

"Any last words, Jackie-poo? Or shall we just get this nasty business over and done with?" Gretel sniffed.

Jack looked at the professor in despair.

The professor gave an unpleasant grin that Jack had never seen before. He reached into his pocket. "Not so fast, Witch."

Gretel sighed. "Really, Merlin? This again?" She raised her wand. "We battled this out ages ago. And you didn't come off very well then, either, did you? Oh well, bring on round two." A beam of blinding light shot from the end of her wand.

The professor ducked and pulled out a tiny ball of light from his pocket. The ball whizzed around in his hands and grew brighter.

A flicker of fear chased its way across Gretel's face.

But the ball of light fizzed, made a sick popping noise, and went black. A pile of ash fell through the air into the professor's hands.

The professor stared in dismay. "No!" he gasped. "I saved it all these years!"

Gretel threw back her head and cackled, making a sound like shattering glass. The sound cracked across the glade like a whip. "Foolish man! Magic has a sell-by date. Or did you forget about that along with all your ancient knowledge when I destroyed your memory? How pathetic. You're not even worth finishing off properly." The laughter on her face died. She turned her back on the professor.

All business, she rolled up her sleeves and began waving her wand. "Time to deal with you now, Jackie. I don't want to miss bingo." She winked.

Grinning, she pointed the wand at Jack. Ariel jumped

from his shoulder with a startled meow. With a yell, he threw himself to the ground and narrowly missed the searing red light that flew from the wand.

Gretel rolled her eyes and stomped her foot. "Honestly," she hissed, "this is just making the agonizing process longer than it should be. Sit still — after all, you might as well get used to it."

Suddenly, there was a tiny snarl. Jack looked up to see Smash running toward him, his arms spread like an airplane.

"Stop! What're you doing, you dumb goblin?" Jack shouted.

But Smash crashed into him, and before he could push the goblin away, Smash had pulled something from around Jack's neck. Astonished, Jack watched the goblin run away with the fairy coal and the vial of mermaids' tears.

Too terrified to figure out whether Smash intended to save the treasures from Gretel or sell them to the highest bidder for candy, Jack stood up and turned back to face her.

Gretel stomped her foot and shrieked, "That's right, little brother, run as fast as your fat legs will carry you — I'll deal with you later!"

She turned back to Jack. "Traitorous little vermin," she complained.

Jack stared, terrified, as she pointed the wand at him again. All the events of the past week rushed into his mind: The horror of Mr. Scrimp running from Smash; the howl of Ariel as she saw herself in the mirror; the fizz of the waves over the stone floor in the mermaids' forgotten castle; the swarm of fairies cheering the lumbering dragon as it tried to roast him to death. Now he was going to be turned into a statue, with no escape from his prison. Alive but frozen for all time.

Then all his thoughts were concentrated on the beam of light in front of him. Gretel had fired the wand again. Her two heads grinned in triumph. In that moment, they were equally ugly.

"No!" The professor threw himself in front of Jack. The beam hit him between the eyes, then bounced off and briefly hit Jack's right leg.

The professor fell to the ground with a horrible thud. He lay stretched out, grimacing, his hands before him. He had been turned to stone.

Jack fell to his knees. "Professor!" he cried, tearing his throat raw. "Why'd you do it?" His eyes filled with tears as he regarded his friend. The professor had taken the curse for himself. It was his final act of friendship.

But then Jack realized something — he couldn't feel his right leg.

Looking down, Jack gasped. His leg had been turned to stone. And it was spreading over the rest of his body.

Gretel laughed hysterically. "That was so great! The silly old goat really knows how to make a scene!" Miming his fall, she shrieked, "No, take me!" She cackled and doubled over, clutching her stomach.

"And what did he achieve?" Cupping her hand, she

pretended to listen to someone. "That's right — absolutely nothing! And, my dear Jackie-poo, speaking of achieving nothing . . ."

She pointed at his leg, and Jack saw that now his hip had turned to stone too.

"How wonderful! This means I have two lovely statues for my poison garden! And all because that foolish old man had to be the hero! Strike a nice pose for me!" Laughing, she spun around and around, dancing with no one at all.

Jack put his head in his hands. *She's right,* he thought. *We would've been better off if the professor had just let her get on with it.*

Gretel's laughter echoed around the glade. Jack didn't look up. He just concentrated on ignoring the horrible sensation in his side which was growing stronger with every second.

In despair, he rolled toward the tree. Smash was standing underneath it. Frantically, Smash waved at Jack. He screwed up his face and, with an almighty effort, croaked, "Jaaaack . . . cooooome . . . heeeeere . . . tooooo . . . meeeee."

Jack was astonished.

Smash began to jump up and down, beckoning for Jack to come to him.

Jack whipped his head around. Gretel was still dancing, looking demonic in the light. She stopped, took a deep breath, and turned back toward Jack. "Wasn't that fun? But I think my spell is taking a bit too long. I'd really like to make it home in time for a bite to eat. Let's see if we can speed things along, shall we?" She raised her wand.

Suddenly a ball of fur flew through the air. Hissing and spitting, Ariel landed on Gretel's hand — and bit down hard.

"Agggggghhhhh! WHY CAN'T YOU ALL JUST LET ME GET ON WITH IT?" Gretel screamed. "I'll kill you once and for all, you meddling, eyeball-stealing FISH!" She jumped up and down and whirled around and around. But Ariel clung on. Drops of blood splattered through the air.

Jack realized this was his only chance. If he couldn't do something, then he and his friends would die. He took a deep breath and began to crawl. His leg was dead weight. The sensation was spreading up his side and with each inch he crawled, another part of his body went numb.

Behind him, he could hear Gretel's shrieks of pain.

With agonizing slowness, Jack crawled toward the tree. He could feel sharp stones scratching his stomach. But he had to try to reach it. Even if there was no answer there, he had to do something.

Then he heard Ariel wail. He whipped his head around and saw her fly though the air. She landed with a heavy thump on the ground. She didn't move.

Gretel held her injured hand and jumped in circles. "Ouch, that really stings!" she cried.

Sweat dripped into Jack's eyes and his right arm began to go numb. The whole right side of his body had turned to stone. Taking a deep breath, he faced the tree again. He used his left arm to pull himself along. Gripping the grass, he had to bite his lip hard to stop himself from crying out at the pain of heaving his heavy body along the ground.

He reached the tree and turned to Smash. "What is it?" he asked desperately.

Smash held up the fairies' coal in one hand and the mermaid's vial of tears in the other. He gnashed his teeth and growled at Jack.

Confused and frustrated, Jack could only stare. "I don't understand what you mean," he cried.

"Smmmmmaaaashhhhh!"

"Yeah, yeah, that's your name. Anything else?" he asked desperately.

The goblin jumped up and down, miming banging the two objects together. "SMAAAASSHHHHH!" he howled.

"Smash what?" Jack cried

A clear voice rang out in his head. "Oh, come on! Really? The goblin has pretty much spelled it out for thee!"

He saw for a split second the face of the white witch hover in front of his eyes. She gazed at him with a small smile on her lips and radiated calm. She tutted. "Use thy brains and smash them!"

"Smash them? I don't get it!"

"Come on, do show a bit of spirit Jack. Thou art human, after all." She disappeared with a pop.

"Oh!" he exclaimed.

It all clicked into place.

In that instant, he knew.

CHAPTER 25

THE WIZARD'S APPRENTICE

Water and spirit must bring fire to where earth and air meet.

I'm the spirit, he thought with wonder. *That's just an old-fashioned word for someone with a soul, which is me.*

Where earth and air meet. That's the tree! he thought. The fairies had given him the answer in their riddle. *A tree joins the earth and the air together.*

And I have the coal that contains fire.

And the vial holds water.

He realized there was only one way to bring all four together — the way to fulfill the prophecy had been in the goblin's name all along.

Smash.

Jack pulled himself up and grabbed the coal. With a cry, he hurled it at the tree. The coal smashed open. Fire leaped out and the tree began to burn.

"No!"

Gretel dropped her injured hand. She shrieked and ran toward Jack. Her eyes were wide with fear, and her mouth hung open in disbelief. Her second head screamed in pain, its face contorted into a horrible grimace of agony.

With a triumphant cry, Jack wrenched the vial of tears from Smash. The tree was ablaze and flames shot into the air around them. Ignoring the heat, Jack used the last of his strength to throw the vial at the tree trunk.

It smashed open.

Gretel began to howl. It was a horrific sound.

Endless water flew out from the vial. It swirled around the flames, which did not go out. It turned the flames an icy blue, giving off an intense heat that singed the grass black and made the flowers shrivel and die. The tree seemed to grow in front of Jack's eyes, ablaze with flames and death.

Jack remembered where he had seen it before — Stonehenge. "It's fairy fire," he breathed.

It grew, reaching toward the sky, while Gretel wailed and wailed behind him. She clawed at her face and beat the ground.

Then the flames turned icy white. They seemed to be sucked into the middle of the tree. The flames howled and screamed, then, with a cracking sound, they disappeared inside the tree trunk.

All was quiet.

But then Jack heard a sound that he had hoped he would never hear again. He shrank in panic.

A faint buzzing, like an angry hive of wasps. And a deep, muffled drumbeat from far away.

The fairy folk were on the move.

Jack yanked Smash out of the way with his one good arm. The fairies burst from the center of the tree. Screeches filled the air as thousands of the deadly creatures poured into the glade.

Gretel was on her knees, her hands over her face. She started to rock back and forth, moaning.

"Finally," said the fairy king, "we are here to collect your debt, pitiful human witch."

The fairy king hovered at the front of the swarm, his eyes hard and cruel.

Jack was now almost entirely made of stone. He could feel the cold creeping up over his chin. Fighting to keep his eyes open, he watched as the fairy king raised one skinny arm.

A jet of blue light flew from the fairy king's finger. It shot over the glade and wrapped around Gretel. Her one eye bulging, she began to cough.

The blue light grew darker and wrapped itself tighter.

With a grisly popping sound, her young fake head disappeared. The second ancient head fell onto her shoulders.

She then seemed to shrink as her true form was revealed. Bent over like a crone, her body twisted into a skeleton covered with brown leathery skin.

Screaming, Gretel raised her hands in front of her face. They were gnarled like tree roots.

The fairy king grinned. Behind him, the fairies started to hum.

Yanking on the jet of blue light, the fairy king pulled Gretel into the air. Gretel bawled and writhed, but the blue light held her firmly. The fairies all turned and flew back into the tree, dragging the screaming Gretel with them. She disappeared inside. The last Jack saw of her was her combat boots wildly kicking before she disappeared from sight.

As the last of the fairies went through the hole in the tree, it turned to face Jack. With a spiky grin, it saluted and then snapped its fingers. The hole disappeared, sealing the fairies and Gretel inside forever.

Smash leaped up from the ground and hugged Jack. "JackJackJackJack — YYYAAAAYAAAAYYYY! Jaaaccckkk oookkkaaayyy."

And Jack realized that he could feel the hug.

He looked down. He was no longer made of stone. The cold was creeping back from his face, and his body had gone back to normal.

His eyes snapped up. In front of his him, Smash began to change. His face became rounder and he expanded like a balloon. Jack blinked. Before him Smash slowly turned back into a young (and admittedly, rather chubby) boy.

"Hansel!" Jack cried.

"The curse has been lifted, m'boy. You have done well."

Whipping his head around, Jack saw a strange man. Where the professor had been standing was a tall man with faint blue tattoos on his cheekbones. They swirled under his eyes and down to his chin. He wore a long brown cloak and had gleaming white hair down to his knees. In his hand, he carried a long staff with a milky crystal set into the top.

"Don't be frightened. It's me, the professor." He raised one white eyebrow. "Or should I say, Ambrosius Merlin."

Confused, Jack stood up and took one step toward him.

Still he hesitated — was this really the professor, or was he someone else?

Then Hansel laughed and ran toward the professor, who swept him up in a huge hug, lifting the boy off the ground.

Smiling, Jack raced toward them and nearly knocked all three of them off their feet.

They linked arms and jumped around, crazy with joy to be alive.

Jack stopped. "Prof—er, Merlin, Ambrosius-thingamabob. Whatever! Where's Ariel?"

Hansel tapped Jack on the shoulder. Turning, Jack saw a sight that he knew would stay with him forever.

In the middle of the glade was a swirling vortex of water. The three mermaids were floating in the middle, silently watching Ariel through glassy, alien eyes. The cat was lying on the ground, where she had fallen. Her breathing was shallow. Jack started to move toward her.

The professor grabbed him. "No, wait. Just watch."

There was a blinding flash of lightning. A scorched smell filled the air. Jack threw his hands up to shield his eyes.

Dazzled, he blinked. Ariel the cat was gone. In her place was a mermaid. Her skin was gray and, just like her sisters, she had webbed hands and gray orbs for eyes.

Ariel flung her head back and gave a shriek of triumph. With a flick of her tail, she propelled herself forward and used her arms to drag herself toward the swirling water. Her three sisters reached for her, clutching her hands. When they touched, the water shot into the air. They were gone. All that remained were drops of shimmering water, falling gently through the air.

"All the spells that Gretel cast have been broken."

Jack looked back at the professor.

"I will return to wandering the world. Now I'm free, I can access my old magic. Who knows — maybe I'll find another young person to become king or queen of this land. Another King Arthur, perhaps?" The professor reached out a hand. "Will you come with me, lad? We could smite your country's government and take the people back to a time when kings and queens reigned supreme. Just imagine what it would be like to have jousts and feasts in the houses of parliament!"

"Uh, I don't think you should do any smiting. We don't really do that these days."

"Oh yes, of course." Merlin cleared his throat. "I doubt I will ever really get used to modern sensibilities. Anyway, we could still bring about some wondrous deeds, full of mystery and magic. How about it?"

Jack took a deep breath. If he left with the professor — no, he corrected, with the wizard Merlin — he would have many more adventures. The world was full of hidden creatures and places, fantastic magic. For a moment he was tempted by such a life.

But he said, "Nah. I just want to go home."

Merlin scowled. "But you don't understand, m'boy! I'm asking you to be my apprentice. You could become a mighty wizard." A faint blue light began to glow around the professor's head. Jack realized that his power was returning. Merlin seemed to grow larger and more frightening in front of his eyes.

"I know." Jack paused. "Still. I just want to go back to my normal life."

Merlin roared with laughter. Jack recognized his old friend in that moment.

Hansel joined in, his chubby face growing pink.

Jack scowled. "What? What's so hilarious?"

"Nothing." Merlin wiped his eyes. "Absolutely nothing, my lad. It's just that you're such a ridiculously, well, normal boy for a hero who has just saved countless generations of children from a wicked witch!"

"Hmmm." Jack wasn't sure if he thought that was so funny.

Smiling, Merlin gently put one hand on Jack's shoulder. "Thank you, young warrior. Thank you for everything and for remaining true to yourself through all this. Power is hard to resist, yet you seem content to live your life as it should be. That is a humbling lesson you have taught me."

Jack didn't really know what he meant, but he said, "Um, thanks, Prof— I mean, thanks, Merlin."

With a grin, Merlin raised his hands, palm up. Lightning again cracked in the sky, splitting the clouds in two.

Jack jumped, covering his ears.

Merlin began to chant in a strange and rough-sounding language.

The air began to hum in the same way it had when they were at Stonehenge. But this was louder. Jack could feel the humming in his bones.

Merlin began to fade. Jack stared down at his own hands and realized that it wasn't Merlin who was fading — it was him. He was being sent home, just as the white witch had sent him home after he dreamed of the glade. That seemed so long ago now.

"Wait!" he cried. "Will I see you again?"

"Oh, I'll be around." Merlin grinned. "I'll never be too far away, Jack. And if you ever change your mind, I'll always have an opening for an apprentice. Think about it, m'boy. . . ."

* * *

When Jack opened his eyes, he was lying on the pavement in front of his house. The rain was steadily pattering into his eyes. With a start, he sat up. It was almost night. Jack stood up, wincing against the pain in his muscles.

The air in front of him shimmered. For a second, he

257

thought he could see the faint outline of the white witch. Instead of the gleaming white outfit and emerald cloak, she was wearing a pair of simple woolen trousers and a tunic. Her hair was pulled back from her fresh face.

"Oh, hello, you're back! Thanks for all your help. I'd definitely be a statue by now if you hadn't come and yelled at me a few times," Jack said.

She smiled and waved, then the rain started to come down harder. She disappeared in the shower of raindrops.

He realized that, for the first time since his whole adventure had begun, he was alone. There was no Ariel purring round his ankles, no Smash screeching to be fed.

He felt lonely. His friends were gone, perhaps never to be seen again — he'd never even had the chance to say goodbye. And he was just a normal boy again with no quest to follow, no evil spells to break.

Then he felt a shiver go down his spine. Jack just knew that someone, somewhere was watching him.

At that moment, his phone buzzed. He opened it and saw a picture of a McDonald's sign. **Football and burgers tomorrow?** the message from Ayo read. Jack smiled and replied, **Yep. Done with community service.**

Two seconds later, his phone buzzed again. **Sweet**, read the message.

He smiled. *Perhaps,* he thought, *normal's not such a bad thing to be. And perhaps I can carry on saying some of the things that need to be said. I'm kind of a warrior now. Well, -ish.*

He leisurely walked to his door, opened it, and went inside. He was finally home.

* * *

On top of a lonely hill, the wizard and his apprentice watched Jack in a glowing crystal ball that hovered in front of their faces. The apprentice had pink, chubby cheeks and was wearing a long robe that was far too big for him and pooled around the floor at his feet.

They watched as Jack walked up to his father. Mr. Riddle was sitting in his favorite chair, the TV remote on his knee.

Jack asked his father something.

Mr. Riddle looked surprised, then pleased. He nodded, went to grab his coat, and the two of them left the house.

They walked down the road, chatting, before reaching a small shop with a neon sign. It read *Kismet Indian Restaurant*. The pair went in, and the door let out a golden light before closing gently.

"Well," the wizard sighed, "I'm glad that's all dealt with but still, it's such a pity. Jack had a lot of potential." Fixing his new apprentice with a beady eye, he said, "Let's see if we can make a legend out of you instead, eh?"

Hansel grinned. "Long live the new wizard!"

What, you thought that was the end?

REALLY?

What did I tell you about real fairy tales?

There are no happy endings. Jack may have escaped his fate, but the ancient rules of magic still demand a sacrifice.

Yes, I know — I really should let you go back to your cozy life.

But before we go, listen to that noise on the wind. Can you hear the fair? And look, you can see the flashing lights in the distance. Let's go see the big rides with the thrillingly rickety carriages. The bumper cars that slam against each other, knocking the breath from your lungs. The smell of cotton candy sticky in the air.

HERE WE ARE.

There's the Ferris wheel reaching up to the dark heavens. Look closely at the rides on the far edge. The ones standing in the shadows, all lost and forgotten.

Few people venture there.

Look at the wooden carousel, its horses slightly old-fashioned and staring with wide eyes. They seem to be staring right at you. Look closely at the bottom. Is there a crust of soil clinging to the edges, almost as if it has walked here itself? There is? How fascinating.

Now look at the women riding the horses. See their tall hats? And aren't they wearing an odd combination of combat boots and ball gowns? The music is a bit weird too. Instead of loud pop music, it's pipe music.

BA-BA DA-BA DUM DUM DUM,
BA-BA DA-BA DUM DUM DUM.

Watch the carousel slowly start to move. The horses are jerking into motion, unsteadily at first, now smoothly as the giant spoons inside mix the potion.

THE SPELL HAS BEGUN.

Time for you to join them, my friend. I never promised I'd keep you safe on this journey. . . .

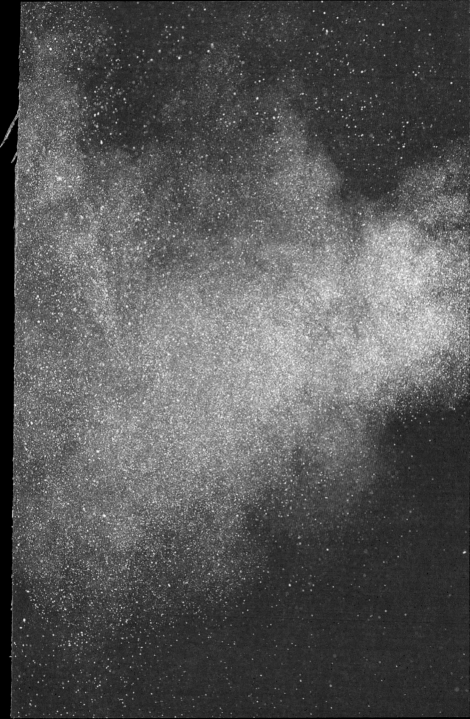

ABOUT THE AUTHOR

H. Easson grew up in England where she spent her childhood searching for the fairies at the bottom of the garden. She is a now a freelance writer and an English teacher living in Hobbit-Land (aka New Zealand) with her husband. *The Legend of Jack Riddle* is her debut novel.